KNOCKED UP AND PUNISHED

PENELOPE BLOOM

1

MILEY

A m I really going to do this?

My heart is thumping, my hands are clammy, and I can't seem to catch my breath, but I'm here. I told myself if I just drove here, maybe the conviction would melt away. Maybe I'd realize how ridiculous I'm being and just go home--back to waiting for the next handsome tragedy to come walking into my life.

When I close my eyes I can still hear the sound of his shouting last night. I can feel the hot sting of pain on my cheek and the slow afterburn of shame that followed. His words still linger in my mind like poison. *Fucking cry. That's all you're good at.*

My hands clench and my eyes sting, but I hold back the tears. I push them back with the force of my anger alone. I won't cry over him. I don't care how much pain he caused me or that my eye is still dark and bruised from when he hit me. He doesn't get any more of my tears.

I told myself I would stay away after Cade. He called himself a Dom and he called me his submissive. I trusted him to show me the kind of relationship I've craved in the deepest corners of my mind. Instead, he took advantage of me and abused me.

So I'm swearing off dominant men. But after one look at my overdrawn bank account, I can't give up my job at the club. It pays triple what I could get anywhere else. Besides, my brother, Kyle, will be there to keep an eye on me, and if Cade has the nerve to show his face at the club again, I'll just stay near Kyle until he's gone.

I let out a slow, shuddering breath.

I can't think about Cade. I won't. It only makes me feel stupid and embarrassed. Ashamed, even, that after all this time I still can't seem to pick the right guy.

I approach the front doors of the building, which is planted between an Italian restaurant and a abandoned movie theater. Two bouncers stand in front of the door in dark suits.

"Is Kyle here tonight?" I ask one of the men, whose name I still haven't learned.

"Yeah," says the taller of the two. "He's working the floor tonight."

"Thanks," I say, slipping inside the door they open for me.

The interior of the club has an old speakeasy kind of atmosphere. A huge bar dominates the main room, and several staircases and curtained doorways extend beyond the main entryway. The men and women in the club are dressed in sleek and elegantly classy clothes that make my own outfit feel too simple and bland, but it's the best I could put together with my budget. Some people wear masquerade style masks, but others make no effort to hide their faces. The club even *smells* expensive- -like fancy liquor and cologne. Music thumps through the air that can only be described as erotic. The beat is driving and moves through everyone in the room, from the way the women move their hips as they cross the room to the way couples gyrate on the dance floor.

I feel so out of place here, but something draws me to this world. It's like an invisible string that I can't break free from--the farther I move from it the tighter the pull gets until I end up here again.

I tuck some hair behind my ear and start walking through the crowded club, unable to stop from brushing shoulders with people as I go. I find Kyle leaning against a wall by the bar. He's wearing a tight black shirt and has a bored look on his face. He smiles when he spots me, but his expression falls when he notices my black eye.

He pushes off the wall and rushes toward me, concern written all over his face. "Where is he?" he asks.

"Stop," I say softly. "I appreciate it. But I don't want you to go trying to kick some client's ass. We both need our jobs."

"You think I care more about my job than my little sister?" His eyes are hard and piercing, already scanning the crowd for Cade.

"Kyle," I say, putting my hand on his arm. "I just need you to keep him away from me if he comes back. Okay? Please let me try to fix the rest. Maybe I can convince the owner to ban him or something. But I need to do it myself," I add more quietly.

He watches me for a long time before letting out a long breath and nodding, jaw clenched tight. "But if he tries to lay a hand on you, I'm going to break his fucking arm off."

"Fine," I say with a small smile. "Do you know anything about the owner?" I ask.

"You haven't met him?"

"You have?" I ask, a little surprised. "I've only been allowed to meet the bouncers and the bartender since I started. I'm not even supposed to go into any of the rooms beyond the lobby yet."

Kyle purses his lips thoughtfully. "Probably for the best. It gets... uh... kind of intense in some of the rooms. I don't know if I like the idea of my little sister going into those places."

I plant a hand on my hip and glare at him. "Really, Kyle? You're fine with me getting a job at a BDSM club and even dating one of the clients, but you don't like the idea of me *going into those places?*"

"Hey, I never said I liked this, but at least you're just bartending in the lobby. I can keep the creeps at bay when you're out here. You start going into the scene rooms and the exhibition areas and you'd be on your own."

"Is that where the owner is? In one of those rooms?"

"His office is way in the fucking back. And..." Kyle sighs, shifting on his feet and leaning in closer. "Just be careful, okay? I get a vibe from that guy. I don't know if it's good or bad, but just be careful."

I nod, resisting my inner-teenager's urge for a dramatic eye-roll. I know Kyle is just trying to protect me, so I can't be too annoyed with him. He has been my shield for as long as I can remember. Back when our dad's abuse changed from emotional to physical, Kyle was there to be my protector.

I leave the bar area for the first time since I started working here and head in the direction Kyle said--toward the back, where dark red curtains are all that stands between me and the mysterious back of the club.

I push through the curtain into a large room set up like a private theater, with sleek, half-backed couches positioned all around the walls in a semi-circle. A raised section of the room serves as a stage. There is a line of men waiting off to one side of the stage and a woman standing in the center of the stage, her head hidden behind a lace hood. Besides the hood, she's completely naked and tied to a tall post by several leather straps. She probably couldn't move a muscle if she tried. The way she's positioned has her legs spread and her ass tilted up in the air, giving the masked man standing behind her access to slide his fingers inside her. The sounds of her moans fill the room, drowning out the low music. After a few moments the man backs away and another man approaches from the awaiting line.

I take a half-step back, suddenly feeling in way over my head. *This is insane.* Those people are just waiting in line to have their turn with her like it's some kind of buffet. I keep backing away from the scene in front of me until I bump into the wall and suck in a startled breath.

I've never thought of myself as a prude, I mean, I've always felt drawn to the lifestyle, but this is... overwhelming. I feel extremely uncomfortable, a little disgusted, and a whole lot curious. Like crane my neck to look at a train wreck kind of curious.. This curiosity feels dark and lust-filled and has me imagining what it would be like to stand on that stage with lace covering my head, waiting in total anonymity while strangers objectified me and *used* me.

I shiver.

Maybe in another life.

I turn to leave but stop short when I come face to face with a masked man. He's tall. *God is he tall.* I have to crane my neck to look up at him. The parts of his face I *can* see are strong and angular: a jaw dusted with stubble, defined chin, and eyes as gray as stormclouds watch me from within the mask. My eyes wander down his neck to the broad shoulders beneath his suit.

Nothing good. There's nothing good that can come from a man like this. I've made that mistake enough times in my life, and maybe for once I can actually learn my lesson. *Just leave. Walk away before you get tangled up with another asshole. Before you get hurt.*

"Excuse me," I mutter quickly. Even as I speak, I can feel the traitorous flame deep inside me flickering to life, daring me to see what this masked man has to offer. That's a dangerous, stupid thought, though. I came here to find the owner and talk to him about Cade, not to get myself entangled in another disaster waiting to happen.

I sidestep and try to move past him, but he blocks my path. "I never said you could leave, princess," he says in a deep, rich voice.

Wrong night to test my patience, asshole. "Yeah?" I say. "It's good I don't need your permiss--"

My words are cut short when he actually sticks his arm out,

blocking me from passing. "You sure about that?" he asks. "You sure you can get out of here without begging?"

I swallow hard. Fear curdles in my stomach, but I don't want him to see how he's affecting me. "What happens if I scream? Won't those bouncers come drag you out of here?"

He watches me without fear. "We could find out." He steps closer until his hard body presses against mine, until I can smell his cologne. So close I'm practically enveloped in his big, strong body. "Go ahead," he whispers. He plants his hand on the wall above me and leans down until his lips are beside my ear. "Scream for me. I'm sure it'll just be the first of many."

I clench my teeth, breathe out a frustrated but determined breath, and then stomp down on his foot as hard as I can. He grunts in pain and flinches back with a curse of annoyance.

I shove the curtain aside and head for the exit. The owner will have to wait. Maybe forever. This was a mistake. Coming back here was a mistake. I don't care how good the money is. I don't care how much my soul seems to cry out for the kind of intimacy I imagine can only be found in a dominant-submissive relationship. I need to close this chapter of my life and leave it where it belongs. *The past.*

The sound of my heels stomping across the floor draws a few looks, but no real serious attention. No one even looks close enough to see the tears ruining my mascara. I guess it's all just hitting me full force tonight--how far I've let things get out of my control. How completely lost I am.

I'm storming toward the exit when a firm hand grips my arm, stopping me in my tracks. I see Kyle rushing toward us from my peripheral vision, ready to clock whoever this asshole is.

The masked man sees him coming too. Instead of bracing himself for the punch, he lifts his mask, which stops Kyle's attack as surely as if he had run into an invisible wall.

"Mr Carlyle..." Kyle mutters. "Ah, sorry, sir. That's just my sister, and--"

"And she's perfectly safe with me. You can go back to your post. And *you*," he says, turning those stormcloud eyes, intensity radiating from him like heat, on me. "*You're coming with me.*" His voice is flat and hard, leaving no room for argument, no room for protest. To my surprise, even Kyle steps back slightly, apparently ready to let me leave with this man.

"There's a place we can talk more privately."

I think about stomping on his foot again for the way he talked to me in the other room, but whether it's a combination of being caught off guard by how disarmingly gorgeous he is or something I can't comprehend yet, I feel compelled to follow.

I decide to bottle up all the snarky, sassy things I want to say right now and play nice. I need to be calm, maybe I can convince this man to ban Cade and then I might just be able to stay working here. "I didn't get your name," I say as politely as I can.

"Jayce," he says, taking my arm and leading me back the way I came.

He clutches me as we walk, it's like he's afraid I might fly away. Like he doesn't ever plan to let me go. Guilty pleasure swirls in my chest from his touch. Jayce is a total stranger to me, but there's something comforting in the possessive way he's holding me. I've been with possessive men before, but the way he holds me feels protective instead of restrictive. It makes me want to cling to this moment until he's erased the pain of my past. The way he holds me makes me feel like a coveted prize. Before now, I've only ever been held as if I were a thing--just a prisoner at the mercy of my captors, waiting to be used for their every whim and without any care for my wellbeing.

Just a few words and a few moments with Jayce and I'm already comparing him to past boyfriends. This is *exactly* why I get into so much trouble. I'm so desperate to be loved and needed that I cling to the first sign of attention any guy gives me, and apparently I attract jerks like flies on shit.

I barely notice where he's taking me until we're inside a room lit entirely by blue light. Some kind of fog or smoke rises slowly from the metal grating beneath our feet. A padded table with straps and cuffs sits in the center of the room, and huge blocks of ice are positioned by the walls. I frown in confusion, trying to piece together what the purpose of this room is and failing.

"It's freezing in here, why...?"

"Sorry," he says. "It's busy tonight and this is the only open room right now."

"You don't have an office or something?" I ask.

The corner of his mouth twitches up a fraction. "It's being remodeled."

I narrow my eyes at him before wandering slowly through the room, trying to compose myself. I find a vent blowing warm air near the large window that takes up an entire wall of the room. I can see a few couples lounging in booths on the other side. They aren't paying us any particular attention, but I'm sure with the vibrant blue light in here, they could see us clearly enough, except for what little privacy the fog might give.

"I feel like an animal inside a zoo here," I say.

"Or a piece of art on display," he suggests. "Something beautiful to be admired and desired, to be lusted after. He folds his arms and regards me. I feel naked beneath those eyes, as if he's stripping me not just of my clothes but my emotional armor, seeing down to the very core of my being. His gaze settles on my black eye. A change flickers across his face. My brother has always been protective of me, but the look on Jayce's face seems like he's ready to kill someone. "Who did this?"

He moves closer, putting his fingertips to my cheek in such a delicate, concerned way I find myself taken off guard.

"That's what I was actually here to talk to you about," I say. "He's a member of the club. Cade Sims. I wanted to see if you would--"

"He's done." His words cut through mine like a knife, silencing any doubt or fear I might have that Jayce wouldn't do anything about Cade. "He'll never step foot in my club again." He rubs his thumb across my lips, sending chills down my neck and making my breath catch. "He'll never touch you again."

"I should go," I say quickly. I try to push away, but he doesn't budge.

"Why are you always trying to fly away, little bird?" he asks with a wicked grin.

I point to the bruise and give him a dry, unamused look. "Take a wild guess."

"Let me show you," he says softly, still not letting me move. "You're hard on the inside. I can see it." His palm moves to my chest where he presses his fingertips, eyes never leaving mine. "You've been hurt. *Scarred.* But I can help you heal."

"You don't even know me," I snap with more anger than I intend.

"Do you want it to stay that way? I'll know if you're lying," he adds.

I believe him. I don't know why or how. But it really does feel like he's looking straight through me--as if I'm laid bare before him. No secrets.

"I don't know," I say. It's the truth, or as close to the truth as I can manage to get, even in my own head.

"You're scared." There's something soothing in his voice. It's deep. Rich. And the vibrations settle into me like massaging fingers, easing some of the tension from my muscles. "You're afraid to trust again." His hands are moving now, exploring me.

I'm conscious of how we're standing in front of a window where dozens of people can watch us, but somehow I can't move that realization from the back of my mind to the front. Jayce is taking up all the space.

"Let me show you how a real man treats a woman. Let me show you what it feels like to be coveted. To be claimed. *To be owned.*"

His words intoxicate me. He reaches into the very essence of me, pulling out my fears and holding them up to the light, eradicating them with the heat of his breath alone. Every syllable erodes my conviction to fight, my will to struggle.

"This is crazy," I breathe.

"Crazy would be letting you go," he says, lips brushing my neck. "I knew I needed to taste you when I saw you. I want to know what it feels like to call you mine. To dominate you."

"Take me," I say, shocked by how quickly he was able to batter down my defenses, but maybe I shouldn't be. My heart feels like a gaping wound after yesterday, and Jayce is offering me a distraction, maybe even a soothing balm to take away some of the pain. "Just this once. Just for tonight. Take me away from it all."

His body is against mine, lips crashing against my mouth. His weight carries me backwards until I bump against the window, pressed tightly against it and pinned by him. My existence blurs into a tangle of warm lips, strong hands, and the hard pressure of his erection against my stomach. For a few blissful moments, I let go. I stop thinking about Cade. I don't think about all the others before him. I forget my dad and his abuse. It all fades until there's only Jayce and his touch, only the places where our bodies collide.

"Jayce," I say, "People will see us."

"Let them see. I'll show them how you belong to me. How sweet your submission is and how jealous they should be that it's mine."

I close my eyes, breathing out the tension and last threads of resistance I feel. I want it. It may only be temporary, and it may not mean anything to him beyond a meaningless hookup, but I want what he's promising, even if it's just a taste.

"Take your dress off for me, princess. Nice and slow."

I bite my lip, opening my eyes slowly until I can see him standing there in the blue light and surrounded by the smoke lifting lazily up and swirling around his broad form. Desire is written on every inch of his face, and I can't help drinking it in.

He wants me. He wants to see me naked and he wants to *take* me. It's only when I reach down to the hem of my dress and feel the slight tinge of pain from the other places Cade hit me that my self-consciousness takes over. I remember the bruises. I remember what it looked like when I stripped down before my shower this morning and looked in the mirror. No permanent damage. No cuts. No broken bones. Just purple reminders of what a stupid little girl I was for trusting Cade, for thinking I could let him be my dom.

My hands fall to my side and a shiver runs through me, forcing up a well of emotion that makes my eyes prick with the threat of tears. I expect Jayce to be angry, to scold me or yell at me for not obeying, but instead he moves slowly toward me as if I'm a scared animal that might scurry away at any sudden movement.

He tilts my chin up until I have no choice but to look into his eyes. His gaze devours me again and I feel that same sense of being stripped bare again.

I know what the other men I've been with would do. They would get defensive at the sight of my bruises and demand to see what was done to me. They'd rage and make a show of protective violence, trying to prove how different they were, all while still planning to fuck me and use me just the same.

I wait for the inevitable, for him to ask to see what I'm hiding and then to somehow make this about him until I feel like *I'm* the one who messed up.

But he doesn't speak. He carefully puts his arms around me, then kneels slightly to sweep my legs out from under me and carry me to the table in the center of the room. He sets me down like I'm the most fragile piece of glass.

Any words I could say are trapped uselessly in my throat. I can only watch this powerful man move deliberately to the big window, where he presses a button that brings down a thick black curtain covering the entire window.

He lifts the hem of my dress until it's just below the line of my panties, where he sees the first bruise. His brow furrows with anger, but he still says nothing. He reaches beneath the table and opens a drawer. When he stands back up, he's holding a small bottle, which he clicks open and squeezes into his palm. He massages the ointment into my leg. I gasp at the first touch because it's warmer than I expected, and the heat seems to seep beneath my skin until it's inside the muscle itself, but it's soothing, though I think right now I wouldn't care if he was rubbing mud on my legs with those big, strong hands.

"Lift up, princess," he says. Making his intentions clear. There's a commanding tone to his voice, but it's gentle.

I press my feet down and arch my back, lifting my butt from the table, which allows him to pull my dress up and off, exposing me to his gaze and allowing him to see the biggest bruise from where Cade kicked me when I fought back. I can't meet Jayce's eyes. I look away, bringing a hand up to shield my eyes. The shame flows through me too strongly to see his reaction, to watch as he realizes what a weak woman I am to let something like this happen.

He takes my wrist and pulls my hand down by my side again, moving it away from my face. With his other hand, he tilts my face toward him again, locking eyes with me. "This wasn't your fault. None of this was ever your fault."

Chills spread through my body like ripples in a pond until they settle behind my eyes, where tears well up. My lips twitch uncontrollably as the emotion tries to flow out of me. *It wasn't my fault.* It's such a simple idea, so obvious, but I needed to hear it, *God I needed to hear it.*

"I always pick the worst guys," I say in a voice thick with emotion.

He brushes away a tear with his thumb, grinning down at me like he's known me his whole life. "Not always."

I force a little smile. "Somehow I don't think this counts. Whatever *this* is."

"This?" he asks, pouring more lotion into his hand and rubbing it into the bruise on my side. "This is the first time I've ever found a woman I would consider taking as a submissive."

"You can't be serious?" I ask. "You own a BDSM club... you must've had dozens of submissives before."

"Never," he says. His hands work a slow, soothing rhythm at my side, never pressing too hard, as if he's perfectly in tune with my body and my needs. "I'm a very particular man, and I have very particular tastes. I guess the right little bird never came fluttering into my window with a broken wing before. *Until tonight.*"

I look up at him, trying to decide if he's telling me the truth or if he's just trying to string me along with some kind of pickup line. "Well, I hate to disappoint you," I say sourly. "But I apparently have terrible taste in men. And I'm starting to like you. So chances are you're an asshole."

He chuckles. "Don't you see the difference? You didn't choose me, princess. I chose you."

I bite back a smile and give him a side-eyed glance. "Are you always this smooth?"

"I'll always be exactly what you need," he says. "Gentle. Strong. *Rough.* Whatever you need."

"Always?" I ask. "Until you've had your fun with me tonight and we go our separate ways, you mean?" I hate that I'm unable to just enjoy this, to let this be an experience and leave my baggage at the door, but every time I think I can forget, it comes washing back into the present, poisoning my thoughts.

"And if tonight doesn't satisfy my needs with you?" he asks. "What do you think will happen then?"

I half-smile. "What are you trying to say?"

"I'm not trying to say anything," he says, smoothly unhooking my bra and pulling it away with a cocky smirk.

I itch to cover myself, but something in his movements and his eyes tells me I'm not supposed to. So I hold my hands still against my self-conscious impulse, letting my breasts feel the cold, open air until my nipples harden into points.

He takes his time admiring my breasts, not touching them, just looking with those breathtaking eyes of his.

"What I *am* saying is that I don't see why I would ever let you go. You're too special. *The perfect catch.*"

A hint of mischief trickles through me at his words, like we're playing some kind of complex game of words that is a precursor to foreplay--or maybe it *is* the foreplay. "Who says you caught me?" I ask.

He's so quick I can't even react before he's fastening one of the restraints on the table around my wrist.

"Hey!" I say in surprise, reaching for the restraint, but he takes my other hand, pinning it while he straps me down.

"Sorry," he says with no hint of remorse in his tone. "I don't want you to get skittish and fly away on me."

"Am I your prisoner now?" I ask. The question makes heat flow between my legs in the dirtiest way imaginable. I would normally think the idea of being held captive, against my will, terrifying or wrong, but I don't. In such a short time I already find myself wanting to trust Jayce, so much that to do anything else is like swimming against the current. Everything about him makes trusting him feel right, like he's the man I've been trying and failing to find.

"I guess that's a matter of interpretation," he says, reaching for his belt and pulling it free in a smooth motion.

"Interpretation of what?" I ask, unable to take my eyes from the bulge in his pants as he strips his jacket and reaches for the top buttons of his shirt.

"Of what it means to be a prisoner, because no, I don't plan to let you leave. But you *are* going to love every moment of your captivity with me." His expression changes just slightly and he leans down until his face is close to mine. "Whoever did this to you," he says, softly touching the skin above the bruise at my side.

"They were a fucking animal. They don't deserve to have a submissive or call themselves a dom. I'm going to show you a real experience--the kind you deserve. So let me make this absolutely clear, princess. Only two words have power from this moment onward. Say 'yellow,' and I'll know you're nearing your limits. Say 'red,' and everything stops. No questions. No guilt. I need to know that you understand me."

"I understand," I whisper. My heart is thudding against my ribcage and my throat feels so tight I can barely breathe. Being in here with Jayce feels as if I'm walking along when the ground suddenly opens up beneath me and swallows me into a rush of pure darkness, where I'm falling away from the world so fast I can't stop--but right now I'm not sure I want it to stop.

He waits for a time, eyes roaming my body like he doesn't have the slightest bit of shame over enjoying the sight of me, and *wow*, I've never felt as sexy as I do under his gaze, bruises, imperfections, and all. He looks at me like I'm a goddess laid out on display for him, like there couldn't be a more perfectly crafted body in all of the world and he's just barely containing his hunger to take me.

When he finally moves, it's to begin stripping his tie and undoing his shirt methodically. When he pulls the fabric away, I suck in air at the sight of him. Every muscle is carved into him, like there's not an ounce of fat on his body. He's made entirely of hard lines and smooth, tan skin. He tosses his shirt to the floor and moves to his pants next. His every movement seems calculated, even the way his eyes flick up to meet mine teasingly just before he reveals even more of his exquisite body. He flicks open the button of his pants and lets them fall until he's standing before me in nothing but his tight-fitting boxer briefs, which are doing a poor job of hiding the size of his huge cock.

My eyes trace its length with more than a little trepidation. I've never had something that big inside me, and I'm not sure it'll fit, but the thought of trying already has me wet and throbbing.

He hooks a thumb tauntingly in his waistband and waits with a knowing look on his face. He yanks them down in one motion, and his cock springs free. I let my eyes wander the entire package, from his length, to the sharp "V" shaped cuts of his abs, all the way up every inch of hard muscle until I find his face and gray eyes. I expect him to climb on top of me, but instead, he strides back toward the window where he pressed the button to lower the blinds and lets his finger hover there. He turns his head to me, waiting. I realize he is giving me a chance to safe word him, and when a moment turns into several, the faintest hint of a grin touches his lips.

He presses the button, retracting the curtains again.

There are at least six couples and one large group of five or so people standing and sitting just outside the glass. My heart immediately pounds harder, blood rushing to my cheeks. But the embarrassment doesn't come without a white-hot thrill that feels like molten lava just beneath my skin, setting me on fire with both need and desire.

All my worries, doubts, and fears from my past are dulled until they don't seem as important, and for the first time in a *long* time, I feel free. I feel like myself, just stripped of all the extra baggage and weight I carry around with me every day.

Jayce stops at a small box spewing smoke before he comes back. He plucks out a handful of ice cubes and brings them to a small rollaway table beside the table where I'm strapped in tight. He sets the ice down and brushes his hands off before reaching for the restraints near my ankles. He ties them tight and gives a good hard tug until they are so snug I can barely wiggle my legs. For the first time, I feel truly trapped. Before, I could at least entertain the idea that with some creative work, I could use my toes to free my hands, but now? I'm at his mercy.

My fate lies in my trust of him--my trust that he won't give me a reason to want to escape, and that he'll listen when I used the safe words. Unlike Cade...

"Jayce" I say.

"No," he says. "You will call me Sir until told otherwise, do you understand?"

"Yes."

His eyebrow raises in a mixture of amusement and scorn. "Naughty little princess."

"Sir," I say quickly.

"Too late." His lips curl into a smirk. "It's time I teach you how pain and pleasure are really just two sides of the same coin."

He picks up an ice-cube between his thumb and forefinger. I watch the way his warmth immediately makes the ice start to melt down his arm and how the water traces a path across his skin, where it drips from his elbow into the blue mist curling up from the floor.

I'm reminded that we have an audience when I notice movement on the other side of the glass--another couple realizing a show has begun and deciding to stop to watch. I can't say why being watched sends such a jolt of excitement and dirty pleasure through me, but I feel more more sexually alive than I ever have in my life right now. I feel objectified and owned, but with none of the negative context I've come to expect those words to carry. It feels tender and scorching hot at the same time. Everything I ever imagined being a submissive could be made real.

He brings the ice cube just above my erect nipple, waiting with patience as a drop of cold water forms and drips down to my areola. I flinch, momentarily shocked by the cold water but my skin quickly warms it. I think he's going to put the ice to my skin, but he seems to be in no rush. He's watching my face instead, *studying me.*

"Pain is often misinterpreted," he says. "Some do enjoy true agony, but for most, pain is only a tool. Like any tool, it can have horrible results when used wrong." His eyes trail down to the bruise at my side, sending a fresh wave of shame through me.

He notices, and turns my cheek when I try to look away so I'm still facing him eye-to-eye. "I won't ever pretend to know how that must have hurt, princess. Never. I won't pretend I understand the physical or emotional pain of being betrayed by someone you trust. But I will promise you this. I will *never* take your trust for granted. I will cherish it. I'll treat it like the precious gift it is, and a day will never pass that you don't thank God you gave it to me. I swear it."

"And what if I don't trust you enough to believe that?" I ask.

"Sir," he growls. "Don't forget where you are."

"Sir," I add, though not without a defiant bite to my voice.

"Then it's up to me to change your mind, kiss by kiss and inch by inch." He pops the ice cube in his mouth and leans down to kiss me.

It's like no kiss I've ever experienced--like being embraced by some ice king on a distant planet or taken to a cold, dark cave by a barbarian who just came in from a blizzard. It's all my childhood fantasies wrapped into a single, startling sensation. His tongue flicks across my lips, already cold and biting from the cube of ice, and his lips leave chilly memories of his touch everywhere they press against me. The movement of our tongues sends the ice cube from his mouth to mine, where it chills my mouth until the numbness makes the comparative warmth of his mouth a new shock all over again. When the cube eventually melts down between the passion of our mouths, he pulls back, dragging his hand along my jawline as he does.

"Pain doesn't have to be unpleasant. Served up with pleasure, it can have the same effect without any of the discomfort. Or," he says, picking up a another cube and pressing it gently against my nipple. "It can be uncomfortable."

I squirm against the cold after only a few seconds. The mild discomfort starts to transition to a dull, biting kind of pain. I take a deep breath, which only pushes my breast harder against the cube and drives the spear of cold farther into me. Just when I'm about to ask him for mercy, he pulls the ice away and sinks his head down to the spot, where his warm lips feel like fire after the cold of the ice.

I gasp, arching my back and bucking against my restraints. He runs his hot tongue along the edge of my nipple and then sucks the hardened nub into his mouth before lifting his head to smirk at me. "But the discomfort only makes the relief that much sweeter. Doesn't it, princess?"

"Yes," I say breathlessly. "Sir," I add.

He chuckles. "That's good. You're learning." He caresses my cheek, holding his hand there as he leans down to kiss me on the lips just as tenderly. The way he's able to shift from fiery passion to smoldering tenderness is a shock to my system--and not a bad one. It might be easy to get used to his tender touches or even his reckless, passionate touch, but not when I don't know what to expect. It keeps my nerves alive and ready for everything as if they are truly drinking in the world for the first time.

He picks up a fresh ice cube and takes it between his front teeth. I think he's going to kiss me again, but he moves by my feet and starts to--

Oh God.

He climbs on the table and grips my panties in both hands, yanking so the fabric splits down the middle and splays open, lying uselessly beneath me and dangling over the edges of the chair. He lowers his head dragging the ice cube along my inner thigh in a way that makes me jump, but only as much as I can while pinned down.

I've never been as wet as I am now, never felt more blinding need to be filled and *fucked.* He's not going to give me the relief I want, yet. I don't know how I know, except that he seems so supernaturally in tune with my body and my needs that I think he must know exactly how bad I want him inside me right now--how bad I want to cum for him. And I think he's enjoying dragging it out.

He gently sets the ice down just above my clit where it starts to melt against the warmth of my skin, cold rivulets of water trickle down the creases of my inner thighs.

"Pain isn't just about enhancing pleasure," he says.

I squirm, but I'm careful not to move so much that the ice falls from me. Though he didn't say so, I suspect Jayce won't be pleased if I let the ice fall. So even as the cold starts to feel more like a numb, burning sensation, I stay still, looking into his eyes-- using them as an anchor to push past the discomfort.

"It's also about establishing lines of trust. Learn to trust that I know your limits better than you do, and only then can you truly let go. Only then can you truly *submit*."

I close my eyes, biting my lip against the mounting discomfort. He brings his mouth down over the ice, giving me just the barest tease of warmth before he draws a trail from my mound to my clit with the tip of his tongue. He *attacks* my pussy with his mouth like he's been dying to taste me for his entire life. I struggle to spread my thighs more for him, but can only do so much with the restraints. I don't even notice the people watching us anymore beyond the vague awareness in the back of my mind that we're putting on a show and the dirty undertone that it adds to situation.

His touch is fire one second and ice the next, with the heat of his tongue lapping at me only to be replaced by the icy sting of the cube. When the first ice cube melts down to nothing, he lifts his head and I can see the glimmer of my juices on his mouth. The sight of it is so hot I wouldn't be able to stop from tackling him to the ground and taking that cock of his myself if I wasn't tied down.

He picks up another ice cube and gives me a look that makes me nervous, like he's excited about something dirty he's going to do, and if what he has already done wasn't dirty and exciting enough for him, I can only begin to imagine what he's planning.

2

JAYCE

My princess is laid out for me like a treasure. Curling hair as silky and black as raven's feathers, but with the most stunning sky-blue eyes I've ever seen. She's beautiful, but not just because of her curves or the shape of her face. There's a beauty in what lies behind her eyes--the set of her mouth and the way she carries herself. *She's wounded.* I knew it from the moment I saw her. My little bird with the broken wing...

To see something so perfect and pure that has been broken and abused makes my blood boil. It makes me want to hurt. To kill. But more than that, it wakes an unstoppable need in my chest to take her into my care and protect her from any more harm, to give her a chance to heal so the world can see how fucking sublime she is.

She's my perfect stranger. My princess. Whether she realizes it or not, I have no plans to let those long legs walk out of my life. So I'm going to start by giving her a night she'll never forget.

I take the ice cube and hold it up to her. I let the anticipation build. Used properly, anticipation and suspense work just as well as pain and discomfort. They are all tools, and crafting the perfect sexual experience is much like building a fine piece of art-

-something extraordinary can be made with the most simple tools, or even no tools at all, but mastery of every tool can lead to something so exquisite it could have never been previously imagined.

I wait until the flicker of her eyes from the cube to her mound tells me she has connected the dots and knows what I'm about to do. Using the edge of the cube, I take my time drawing a line from her bellybutton to her entrance, where I apply just enough pressure to ease the cube inside her. They are small cubes, roughly the size of a bottlecap, and I know her heat will make short work of them, so I don't stop yet.

She's watching me with fascination, eyebrows pulled together and mouth open. I can already see the way the ice is melting and running out of her pussy in a thin line of water. I can hardly wait to lick it up, but I want her to have the full experience, so I don't stop yet.

I tease her with each cube, tracing wandering paths across her body and sometimes following with my mouth to give her the contrasting sensation she needs, but one by one, I get five cubes of ice inside her pussy.

I can't deny myself anymore, so using the flat of my tongue, I lick up her thigh where the water has run from her pussy all the way up to her clit, loving every fucking second of it. She cries out, body rocking against the restraints and eyes squeezed shut.

By now, the cold is likely getting intense, especially for someone who isn't used to this. Thankfully, the cure she needs is one I've been dying to give her since I first laid eyes on her. I yank beneath the table to give her leg restraints enough slack to let me bend her knees until I have her where I want her.

"You're not going to take them out first?" she asks, looking down with sudden panic.

"And spoil the fun?"

I don't give her time to dwell on it as I ease the tip of my cock into her, planting both hands on either side of her head so I can hold myself up and watch the expression on her face.

"You feel it, don't you?" I ask as I work just the first few inches of my cock inside her warmth. I stop when I feel the cold of the ice, not wanting to push it deep inside her, only to shock her system with the contrast of the heat of my cock and cold of the ice. "The way the cold makes your body tingle all over? How it makes your pussy tighter for me until your walls are practically choking my cock?"

"I feel it," she says, eyes closed and head tilted back.

"Too much of a good thing can make you numb, but just the right amount..." I say, stretching her with another inch of my cock and pushing the remnants of the ice deeper inside her. I let out a grunt of enjoyment as the melting ice makes her walls feel shockingly cold around me. I know it will only be moments before the ice has completely melted, and I'm going to make her cum as she feels heat return to her core. "And you'll cum like you never have before. Give yourself to me for tonight, princess. Surrender your body. Surrender *everything*."

"Yes," she says, breathing heavily. "Yes, Sir."

"Good fucking girl," I growl. The last of the ice drips between our bodies, and I hold nothing back. I thrust into her, bending to suck her erect nipples, giving her even more of the warmth I know her body is craving.

"God," she cries. "Jayce..."

I never find out what she was going to say, because her pussy is like a hot glove gripping me now, and with a subtle adjustment of my hips, I hit her exactly where I know she needs it. The plan was to pull out, to see how gorgeous she looks with my cum covering her tits and stomach, but for the first time with a woman, I lose control. I lose every last shred of restraint. I might be the dominant, but in the moment she's the one dominating my body. I relentlessly plow into her supple body, until the sounds of my pelvis slapping against hers drowns out my every thought.

She cries out in a single, long, unending syllable of bliss. I clench my teeth as my orgasm rocks me to my fucking core. My cock pulses for what seems like ages, filling her with cum as each wave of pleasure rips through me. When I finally pull out, she's still shaking from her own release. I could overload her senses, push her even deeper into her pleasure, but I don't. I ease myself down from the bench, feeling lightheaded.

"Lie still, princess," I say softly when she tries to lift her head to see what I'm doing. "I'm just removing the restraints. I need to make sure you don't have any friction burns, and I'm going to use an ointment that should help with any unseen irritation."

I move to the curtains and press the button, giving us privacy again. Her aftercare isn't something for the eyes of anyone else. This is our moment.

She lowers her head with the slightest hesitation, but seems to understand. I put more lotion in my hands once I've unbound her. I take my time inspecting her inch by inch. I'm not just making sure she is unharmed after our experience, I'm trying to commit every line and curve to memory. "You're a masterpiece," I say as I rub some of the circulation back into her wrist.

She lowers her eyes, but says nothing.

"You act ashamed when you're complemented. Why?" I ask.

Her eyes dart to mine but she looks away again. "I'm not sure."

I grip her wrist a just a little tighter. "You won't lie to me." It's not a question. Not a threat. It's just a statement. It's a reminder for her own sake--that she knows she can't hide anything from me. I don't care if she sees me as a stranger or a one night stand. I refuse to let her hide from me.

She sighs, rolling her head to the side and staring toward the far wall. "It makes me feel stupid, maybe. Naive. Because so many men work their way into my life with shallow compliments. I used to believe them, *like them*, even. But now it just feels like a trap, I guess. Like I'd be stupid to latch onto it and let it mean anything."

I nod. Stepping back into my briefs and pants as I talk. "The heart is a fragile thing. People talk as if the heart can grow tough and resistant to the world, but I've never thought it worked that way. I think we put up walls. We close ourselves off because we want to protect our hearts like our lives depend on it. Maybe they do..."

I hand her her dress, which she takes and slides over her head as she sits up. "If our hearts don't get tough, what does?" she asks.

"This," I say, touching a gentle finger above where the bruise on her side is and then below her eye. "This," I add, pointing to her forehead. "I think your heart is worth protecting, princess. And I don't want to see your beautiful body have to take another scratch in its defense."

"What are you saying?"

"Let me be your shield. Let me be your Dom. I can take care of you."

She laughs, shaking her head while watching the ground. "We just met," she says, but her tone doesn't convince me she's truly objecting.

"And?" I ask.

She glares at me, but somehow it's more adorable than frightening. "And I'd be crazy if--"

"You let me put ice cubes in your pussy and give you the best sexual experience of your life?"

She closes her mouth, giving me a glare that *is* actually a little frightening. "If I told myself this was more than just a hook up. I mean, *God*," she says, putting her palm to her forehead and leaning her head back with a sigh. "I just had unprotected sex with a complete stranger. What was I thinking?"

"You mean that's not a normal Friday for you?" I ask.

"Actually, this is a normal Friday for me. I wake up finding myself in the middle of a relationship I'd do anything to get out of and realize I'm a complete mess and keep making the same mistakes over and over again. See this is what I mean, I make bad decisions when it comes to men. This," she says, pointing to the room as her lips twitch from holding back tears. "This was just my most recent mistake. But I'm not sticking around to see the horrible ending this time. I may be a slow learner, but even I can see this end coming from a mile away. I'm sorry," she says, picking up her shoes and storming out the door.

She slams it behind her, leaving me standing in the middle of the room. I could go after her. I could convince her to stop and talk to me more--convince her I'm different, that being with me wouldn't be the same. That's not what she needs right now, though. She needs time. I may not have the patience to wait long, but I can give her tonight to figure things out. Tomorrow, she's mine again.

3

MILEY

I blow out a long, frustrated sigh as I stand over the stove top. I've got eggs scrambling, bacon cooking, and biscuits cooking in the oven. If that wasn't enough, I have some turkey sausage in the microwave and a chocolate muffin on standby if I make it that far.

When Kyle steps out of his bedroom in our shared apartment, he raises an eyebrow. "Damn, sis. How much do you think I'm going to eat?"

"This isn't for you," I say shortly.

He pauses, rubbing the mess that is his hair. He narrows his eyes, tilting his head and moving closer until I feel like he's going to see exactly what I'm thinking. "The fuck happened last night, anyway? Bates had to cover your shift when you never came back. You didn't get caught up with some creeps in the back, did you?"

"No," I say, swallowing hard. I've never been a good liar, especially not when it comes to my brother.

"Was it Jayce?" he asks. I can see him tensing. As much as I love Kyle for how he protected me when dad was at his worst, I hate that I can see some of dad in him. Kyle may find a more honorable way to channel his anger, but the same rage boils inside him that always boiled inside dad. The difference is dad took it out on his kids.

"It didn't mean anything," I say, letting out the breath I was holding. "It was dumb. I told him we shouldn't see each other again. So you don't need to--"

"That fucking creep," growls Kyle. "Does he know you're barely twenty-three? How old is he? Thirty? More? You're like a fucking kid to him."

"Kyle..." I say. "I told you. I told *him*. It was a one time deal. Just forget it."

Kyle shakes his head, like it's already forgotten. "Yeah, well that's for the best. Apparently he's into some dark shit. Like some really fucked up criminal kind of shit."

"What?" I ask. "He didn't seem like the type."

"You two did a lot of getting to know each other last night?" Kyle asks in a tone that rubs me the wrong way.

"Maybe we did," I say defiantly.

"Well, I guess he failed to mention the human trafficking scandal from a few years ago. Everybody talks about it. They say he was selling young girls to members of his club in some kind of black market auctions."

"How do I know you're not just making this up to keep me away from him? That you're not just trying to decide who I do and don't date?"

"You don't, Miley," he says, voice full of frustration. "But maybe if you thought about it for two seconds, you'd realize I'm the only person in your life who has ever actually tried to protect you."

I know he doesn't mean for them to, but his words bite straight through me. My chin quivers with the threat of emotion. I push it down. I'm not going to be so weak. I can be strong. I can be tough. It's like Jayce said, I can put my walls up.

"Say I believe you," I say after a moment. "Even *if* I was still planning on seeing him again--which I'm not--what am I going to do, just ask him if he's ever participated in human trafficking?"

"Maybe ask around at work tonight. You might be surprised what you hear. Anyway, I'm going for a run. Don't eat all that yourself, you'll have a heart attack."

"If I ever decide to go back," I say dryly as he laces up his shoes and throws on a hat before heading outside.

I snatch up a piece of bacon and bite into it angrily. I feel like a spoiled brat for thinking it, but I wish Kyle would butt out of this one. I've needed him and appreciated his help my whole life, but just once I wish he'd let me deal with my own mess. I already decided to stay away from Jayce, even if I had the hottest dreams of my life starring him last night.

I grab a biscuit, not caring that it's so hot it burns and take a bite out of it that's so big my cheek puffs out like a squirrel stashing nuts for winter. "Stupid men," I say through a thick mouthful of food.

More like stupid me, though. I already made an appointment to get tested for STDs this morning, because I was reckless enough to let him inside me without a condom. It was so easy to justify in the moment. My brain felt like it was floating on a cloud of white light, like the real world was miles and miles away. I told myself the chances of getting pregnant or catching something were so minimal, that I'd regret it if I stopped him and made him find a condom. Now that sunlight is pouring through the windows? I feel like the world's biggest idiot. He could've gotten me pregnant, for all I know. And if what Kyle said about him is true, there's no way I could let a guy like that into my life, let alone my baby's.

My baby.

Excitement mingles with a strong, *strong* dose of anxiety, making me feel so nauseous I can barely swallow down the huge bite of biscuit I took. I made my choice, however reckless it was.

But if by some cruel twist of fate, I *am* carrying his baby? I owe it to myself and my potential unborn child to go back to the club and ask questions. My decision to continue working at the club or not just became an easy one. I need to know if there is any truth to what Kyle said about Jayce.

4

JAYCE

The music of the club pounds through the air, ringing in my ears and vibrating in my chest, but I hardly notice. Ever since last night, my mind has been laser focused on one thing and one thing alone. *My princess. Miley.* I probably should be embarrassed that I had to dig that up in the club's employee records, but fuck it. I couldn't stop thinking about her, and I wanted to know her name.

I've spent my whole life searching for the right woman. For years, it felt like something was wrong with me. Every relationship seemed shallow and pointless. Sex felt like a stiff exercise, an obligation, even. Then I happened to learn about my older brother Leo's interest in BDSM. I wondered if maybe that was the missing piece, if maybe the reason I never seemed content with my relationships was because they weren't the right kind.

So I dove in. It felt right for the first time, like the world resonated with me. The only problem was I quickly developed a sense for what I wanted in a submissive. The bigger problem was as much as I knew there was something specific I was waiting for, I couldn't put it into words. It was just a knowing that nothing and no one was living up to my desires. It became a dull ache in my chest, a longing that never seemed to go away or subside. I tried a few relationships after I stepped into the world of BDSM, but nothing was ever right.

Then I saw Miley last night. It was like the fucking room stood still, like everything stopped mattering in that moment except making her mine--completely and totally. I knew there wasn't anything to stop me from taking her, from showing her the power of what we could have together. I just wish I had the self-control to use a condom. I've always told myself I never wanted kids. My mom got sick shortly after she had me and passed away. I know it's stupid, but I've always blamed myself, like bringing me into this world is what killed her, or at the very least what weakened her enough that she couldn't fight.

If I got Miley knocked up, I'd be scared to death something would happen to her. As much as I might want to become a father, I wouldn't ever risk the woman I love for such a selfish reason. I couldn't survive having everything I want snatched away because of me.

Letting her leave was the hardest thing I've done in a long time, but it was the right move. I could see the pain of Miley's past etched in her eyes. I saw how she's put her trust in the wrong men and had that trust betrayed, how she's been abused, taken advantage of, and forgotten. She needs to understand that she's free. I can't snare her with force. The only way is to let her realize for herself how badly she wants to be mine, to be owned by me.

So I have to wait. And now the wait is almost over, because she'll be coming in for her shift in a couple hours. But I don't plan to let her get much work done.

The club is busier than usual tonight, but I spot Miley's brother, Kyle, as he comes through the front. He's tall and built like he might have been a football player in high school or college. He notices me and changes directions, heading straight for me.

"Jayce--ah, Mr. Carlyle," he says, correcting himself but not sounding sorry for the disrespectful slip. "I wanted to talk to you."

I size Kyle up, taking in the set of his eyes and his posture, doing my best to measure what kind of man he is. I can see that he probably looks after his sister, but there's something else I sense about him--something I'm not sure I like. "About?" I ask, not bothering to hide my irritation. Let him see that I don't like him. I'll get a better sense of what kind of man he is than if I fake a smile and shake his hand.

"My sister."

I raise an eyebrow. "Go on."

"She's already in a relationship. His name is Cade."

"Not anymore. She broke things off with him. She told me as much last night."

Kyle nods his head, laughing humorlessly. "Yeah, I bet she did," he leans close like he's letting me in on a secret. "Look. I love my little sister, but she's trouble. She likes to watch guys fight over her. She'll say whatever she has to, and then her real boyfriend will show up one day with a baseball bat when you're not expecting it." Kyle mimics swinging a bat at my legs.

I want to believe he's lying. I want to believe it down to my fucking core, but a hairline fracture of doubt splits my certainty that I've found the perfect woman. I know I won't act on his words. She deserves more than that, way fucking more. Whatever he says. But I can feel the slight doubt wriggling its way deep into my mind where it will be nearly impossible to pull free.

"Fuck off," I growl. "You think you're protecting her by talking shit about her? You should be fucking ashamed."

An emotion I can't place flickers across Kyle's face, but it's gone in an instant. "I'm looking out for her. I don't want to see her get into any more trouble. *Or get any more innocent guys hurt,*" he adds before turning to walk over to the bar.

I wait with white-knuckled impatience for Miley to show up

for her shift, but when twenty minutes have passed and she still hasn't shown up, my instincts tell me something's wrong.

I pull out my phone as I push my way to the exit and jog to the parking lot. I call the general manager who runs the accounts and payroll for the club and tell him I need Miley's address to send over a package that showed up at the club. He reads it off without question.

I hang up the phone before jumping into my car. I may come barging into her place and make a total idiot out of myself, but she's either missing work because something wrong, or she's avoiding me. Either way, I'm going to find out.

5

MILEY

"You need to leave," I say for what feels like the twentieth time.

I'm standing in the kitchen next to the drawer full of knives and Cade is on the other side of the counter. His hair is disheveled and his eyes look a little bloodshot, but the worst part is the smell. I was only with him a few months, but I quickly learned to associate the smell of booze with danger, and right now it's wafting to me even from several feet away. I still can't believe I thought he was handsome when we first met. But I guess I should know how even the worst men can put on a clean shirt, comb their hair, and flash a charming smile for a few hours--just long enough to lure me in.

"I'm not going to fucking leave without you," he says.

"*Yes,* you are." My voice is as slow and controlled as I can manage. It feels like I'm trying to talk down a wild animal and even the slightest provocation could be deadly. But I'm not letting him intimidate me into going with him. He's going to find out what's in the goddamn drawer behind me if he tries anything.

"Miley. I know I fucked up," he says. He looks at me with a pathetic attempt at puppy-dog eyes, but to me it just looks grotesque, like some kind of monster putting on a mask--nothing in the expression is quite right, almost like it's practiced and forced. "If you give me another chance I can be better to you."

"Another chance?" I ask, voice breaking. The emotion that wells up so suddenly isn't for Cade. *Fuck him.* It's for all the time I've wasted with men like him. All the unlucky circumstances and poor decisions up until this point. Maybe it took the worst one of them all to finally wake me up and make me realize I need to change. "Another chance to kick the shit out of me? To beat me? To abuse me?"

"Careful," he says, dropping the mask of false sorrow so that the cruelty I came to know from him is front-and-center. "I'm trying to do the right thing here, but if you're going to be a *fucking bitch*, well, I know how to get you in line."

I open the drawer behind me and yank a knife free, pointing it toward him. "I swear to God. If you come anywhere near me, I'll do everything in my power to kill you. I swear it," I promise.

Amusement lights his eyes. "Everything in your power? You mean jack shit?"

He takes a few slow steps around the counter, coming toward me. I sidestep, trying to use the counter to keep him as far away from me as possible as we both circle it. We change directions, and the amusement on his face turns to frustration. "You think this is a goddamn game?" He lunges forward, clearing half the counter and putting himself within grabbing distance of me and the knife.

I take a wild swing, missing his hand by inches so that the knife clinks off the countertop and sends a nasty vibration through my hand. I'm two steps toward the door to the hallway outside when someone knocks so hard on the door it sounds like thunder.

"Miley!" calls a deep voice from outside. "Are you in there? Miley!"

"Help!" I shout, but it's all I have time to do before Cade catches me from behind, pinning my arms to my side.

With a loud crash, the door swings open, breaking off its hinges a split second later. I've never been as relieved to see someone in my life as I am to see Jayce push his way inside with those gray eyes somehow seeming as hot as fire.

He assesses the situation in a fraction of a second, faster than Cade's drunken mind can apparently keep up with, and takes one long step toward me before throwing a lightning-fast punch directly into Cade's nose.

His grip on me goes slack, letting me rush away from him and go to the wall. I turn quickly, holding my knife up in case Cade tries to come for me again. But he's already on the ground, lifting his head dizzily and holding his bloody nose. Jayce towers over him, legs planted wide and fists clenched at his side--clearly sending the message that if Cade decides to get up again, he'll regret it.

"You're Cade?" he asks in a voice that sends a chill through me.

"Fuck you, asshole." Cade's voice is thick with what sounds like a broken nose and a mouthful of blood.

Jayce kneels beside Cade, showing no sign of fear at all. Though I guess a man like Jayce has nothing to fear from Cade. It doesn't take much strength to abuse a woman, especially one who makes the mistake of entrusting her submission to the wrong person. I see that more clearly now that the two men are side by side. Cade looks weak, pathetic, and frail. Jayce is thick with power and confidence, making Cade look like a small boy by comparison.

"I saw what you did to her," Jayce says. His voice is calm and frighteningly quiet. He hasn't said a single threatening word yet, but the promise of violence is so clear in his tone that I have to fight my instincts to squeeze my eyes shut.

"I saw the bruises," he continues. "The first I saw was here," he says, mercilessly planting a punch to Cade's eye. Cade's head snaps back and bounces off the floor. He groans, pulling his hands up to cover his face.

A confusing mixture of sympathy and disgust fills me. Cade is as defenseless against Jayce as I was against him, and as much as I've prayed for this moment, to see him get what he deserves and more... it doesn't feel like I thought it would. I think to how it felt to be hit like that and know I wouldn't wish it on anyone. All I really wish is that Cade and men like him would never hurt anyone else. So how can I stand here and feel good about watching him get beat senseless?

"Jayce..." I say. "It's enough, it's--"

"The second was here," says Jayce, who pulls back his leg and kicks Cade hard in the ribs.

Cade folds in on himself, squirming and groaning. I feel like I'm going to be sick.

"Jayce!" I shout, dropping the knife and running to pull back on him, to stop this before he ends up killing Cade.

Jayce turns on me suddenly, and for a moment it's like he's not even there--I only see wild rage in his eyes. But in a few moments, he seems to wrestle back some control, features softening as he looks me over, putting his hands to my cheeks, my shoulders, my sides--searching me for any sign of injury.

"I'm okay, Jayce. He only grabbed me."

"You're sure?" he asks.

"I'm sure. Thanks to you," I say.

Jayce turns to look at Cade again, and I see some of the inhuman anger start to creep back into his features. I take him by the cheeks and turn his face to mine, standing on my tiptoes I kiss him. It's the first thing I can think of to stop him from exacting more revenge on Cade, but even as the passion of the moment threatens to sweep me away, I know I've made a mistake. I can practically feel Cade's eyes burning into us. When I pull back from the kiss, Cade has already shuffled toward the door, face bloody and hands clutching at his side.

"I'm not done," he says before stepping over the broken door and into the hallway.

"I could kill him," Jayce says lightly.

I look at him in disbelief until I realize he's joking.

He flashes a half-smile back at me. "Sorry. Too soon?"

"Yes," I say with a small laugh. "How did you know I was in trouble?"

"You didn't show up for work. I was waiting all day for you to come, then..." He looks slightly uncomfortable for the first time since we've met. Jayce clears his throat before he frowns at me, clearly searching for the right way to ask a difficult question. "You and Cade," he says finally. "Had you really ended things before last night? Before what we did?"

"Yes..." I say slowly, not understanding why he would ask me something like that. "I told you I did."

He nods, but there's a strange look on his face.

"Wait," I say. "Did you talk to Kyle?" I've made a habit of keeping the identity of my boyfriends a secret from Kyle in the past, because he has a bad habit of making up stories to sabotage my relationships. Now, seeing the way Jayce is looking at me and the fact that he questioned what I told him last night has me wondering if Kyle is back to his old crap.

"I did."

"Wow," I say slowly. "What he said about you was probably a lie, too." I'm talking more to myself at this point.

"What?" asks Jayce.

"He said you were charged with human trafficking a few years ago. He was obviously hoping it would spook me into staying away."

"Did it?"

I tilt my head, considering. "Maybe a little," I admit. "But I was going to ask around at work tonight. And then..."

" "And then," he prompts

"What did Kyle tell you?" I ask, changing the direction of our conversation.

"It's not important. I would've only really believed it if I heard it from you."

"That's a lot of trust to put in a stranger," I say with a small smile.

"You didn't feel like a stranger when I was fucking that tight little pussy of yours."

I look away guiltily. "You know that's not what I mean."

He steps closer, putting his hand on my arm. I hate how the simplest touch from him seems to blast away all my well-laid plans to stay away. "Whatever you need, I'll give it. Just ask."

I shake my head, looking down at our feet, wishing I had a magical crystal ball that tells me the right answers. Whether or not I should trust this man when every single time I've ever trusted a man, it's led to me getting hurt--Kyle included. "How do I know it'll be different?" I ask.

I think I might have to explain more, but I can see from the look on Jayce's face that he understands. "Because you feel what I feel," he says softly. "You do. I can see it in your eyes, princess."

I look away, feeling like meeting his eyes for more than a few seconds is dangerous. Looking into those stormcloud gray eyes is like wading out into a riptide. Where every second I stare into them is another step deeper and deeper, until I can feel the tug of the current at my waist, threatening to pull me so deep I'll be swept away.

Right now, that scares me more than anything. "Maybe I feel something. But I've trusted my feelings before, and look where that got me," I say, motioning to the few drops of blood on the carpet where Cade was lying.

"One date," he says. "Give me just one date. You pick the place, the time, everything. If you still feel uneasy after it's over, then you gave it a shot and you won't look back and ask yourself if you made a mistake passing this up."

"Passing this up?" I ask with a grin. "Passing *you* up, you mean?"

He shrugs. "Sounded better my way."

I laugh, then shake my head and sigh. "Please don't make me regret this."

"Not a chance, princess. Just tell me when, and you're going to have the night of your life."

I can't help smiling a little, because the idea that pops into my head is too perfect to pass up.

6

JAYCE

When Miley insisted on driving separately to meet at the place she picked, I wasn't sure what to think. It was only yesterday that I punched out her sleazy ex, but it already feels like I've been waiting weeks to see her again. As much as I'm dying to get her back into the club, or better yet--my personal play room, I know that's not what she needs. Not quite yet, at least. She needs to see that this isn't another mistake, and I'll be damned if I don't prove it to her.

I look up at the place. *Galaxy Golf.* It's a huge, ten story driving range that looms above a green expanse of astro-turf, but there are electronic targets scattered across the range. I looked the place up before we came, and apparently it makes some kind of game out of it. You get more points for hitting the center of the target or for hitting targets farther away, and you get the most points for hitting the back wall.

I have to admit, it sounds kind of fun, even if I'm absolutely shit at golf.

When I finally see Miley walking toward the front of the building, she's flanked by a woman wearing black fishnet stockings, some kind of black coat with metal rings, and enough makeup that she looks like she's about to walk on stage to perform at a rock concert. I feel my eyebrows creeping upwards. *She brought a friend? Fucking seriously?*

My annoyance is forgotten for a moment as I take in Miley. She's wearing tight, dark wash jeans that make her legs go on for days and a short leather jacket over a dark blue corset that pushes her perfect breasts up and shows just the slightest amount of skin at her waist. She's the perfect vision of subdued and sex kitten.

Damn. She's lucky she brought a friend, or I might lose my conviction to keep this date PG. With annoyance, I wonder if that's why she decided to bring a friend in the first place--to keep me honest.

As much as I wish I had her to myself, I have to give her credit for her cleverness.

"You must be Jayce," her friend says. "I'm Darla." Her voice is a surprisingly deep, monotone, and her sleepy eyes never seem to blink.

"I see," I say, looking to Miley. "I didn't realize you were bringing a friend. I could've invited one of my own."

"Yeah," Darla quips. "Maybe you could have set me up with them." She rolls her eyes and walks inside with this strange, stiff posture and slow but forced grace.

I turn to Miley once we have a moment of privacy. "What are you playing at?"

I can tell she's working hard to keep her nerve, but she stares right back at me. "I brought her because I don't trust myself. She'll keep me from doing anything stupid. *And...*" Miley says with mild reluctance. "Darla loves this place."

I look toward her friend with more than a hint of skepticism. "Seriously?"

"What?" Miley asks with a mischievous glint in her eye. "She doesn't look like a golfer to you?"

I chuckle. "Where exactly did you two meet?"

"I've known her since Pre-K. We were both always getting bullied, so it was one of those unlikely allies kind of things."

Miley says it so offhandedly, but I can tell her childhood isn't just a memory to her. It's a scar she carries with her every day. An irrational anger rises up in me at the fact that I'm only now finding her, that I wasn't there to shield her when she needed it most. But I know all I can do is be good to her now and give her the life she deserves, if she'll let me.

"Any of these bullies still around?" I ask. "I could pay them back, with interest, of course."

Miley eyes me. "Don't take this the wrong way, because I know the thing with Cade..." She chews her bottom lip for a second, searching for the right words. "I needed you last night. But having a guy in my life to punch everyone who wrongs me in the face isn't what I need, not in the long run."

"I could always punch them in the neck," I suggest.

She plants a fist on her hip and gives me glare, but she can't keep from grinning a little. "I didn't take you for the type to have much of a sense of humor."

"Well, the first time we met, I was... distracted. And the second didn't exactly seem like the place for humor."

"Distracted?" she asks.

"I had more important things occupying my mind," I say, letting my eyes rove over her body for emphasis.

Her cheeks flush the most beautiful shade of red. I smirk, which makes her take a sudden interest in her shoes. "Sorry. It still doesn't feel like that was me.. I hardly recognize the *me* that did something so... reckless."

"The real question isn't if you recognize her. It's if you liked her."

Miley raises her eyebrow thoughtfully. "Better than the usual me," she says softly. "The usual me seems to only find ways to wind up the victim."

"Don't do that," I say firmly. "You're stronger than you give yourself credit for. You say you needed me last night? Fuck, *Cade* needed me. If I hadn't shown up I think you would've gutted him in the middle of your living room."

She laughs, but the humor quickly drains from her face as she realizes I'm right. "I really do appreciate what you did. I don't know if I properly thanked you. And I'm sorry for how I've been. I guess we just met at a weird point in my life."

"You're apologizing?" I ask in disbelief. "If you haven't noticed, I'm over here jumping through hoops to keep you from running off. The only thing you need to apologize for is being so goddamn irresistible that I'm willing to make a fool out of myself for you."

"You making a fool out of yourself... Now that's something I'd like to see," she says with the first real, full smile I've seen from her.

"Ask and you shall recieve, princess," I say. "Come on."

We go inside, where Darla is waiting by the front doors with her arms crossed. Judging by the look on her face, she ran out of patience about a millisecond after she stepped inside. "Great," she says dryly. "You're ready."

I look to Miley, who gives me a warning look not to antagonize her friend, so I hold my tongue as we get checked in and brought to one of the bays on the top floor, where a digital screen displays the rules and our scores. A few of what I guess are the basic golf clubs are stored at every bay. We also have a table with seating and menus.

"Nice place," I say, looking out over the view of the driving range below. Huge nets stretch at least two hundred or three hundred feet in the air all around the range, protecting the freeway in the distance from rogue golf balls. The sound of clubs cracking into balls rings out all around, and a constant spray of white balls flies out from below and beside us.

"Miley says you're a golfer," I say to Darla, trying to ease some of the awkward hostility that seems to radiate from the woman.

She rolls her eyes at me before walking to the touch screen

panel beside the clubs. She taps her long black fingernails on the screen a few times, grabs a club, and then waves it over a sensor that sends a ball rolling onto a small patch of green near the edge of the driving bay. She gives me a look that I don't think is supposed to be comical--a smug glare is what I would call it--then takes a monstrous swing at the ball.

Her club buzzes over the top of the ball and sends it bouncing twice before it rolls into the net at the edge of the platform.

"Fuck!" she shouts, causing a mom with her young daughter in the bay beside us to cover her daughter's ears and shoot a nasty look our way.

I lurch forward, failing to hold back a laugh as Darla tosses her club down and stomps over to take a seat at the table. "Shoulder injury," she says flatly. "My swing hasn't been the same since last January."

"I see," I say, but I still can't keep the amusement from my voice or my face. Miley seems like she's able to hold her own composure until she looks at me, which causes her to almost burst out laughing.

"Your turn," she says shakily, barely holding in a laugh.

I grab the biggest club I can and look down the range toward the back wall, where I imagine it won't be *that* hard to hit the thing. After all, I'm holding a big ass metal stick... how hard can it be?

I wind up, swing as hard as I can, and hear a disappointingly quiet sound as I barely catch the edge of the ball and send it careening so far to the right that it hits the net at the edge of the range.

I sigh, laughing a little at myself. "Guess there's a reason people practice this," I say, handing the club to Miley, who takes it and moves to line up her shot.

She sets up in a way that makes me think she might actually know what she's doing. She pulls back the club and even my untrained eye can tell she's about to hit a great shot. Sure enough, the sound rings out, putting my own dinky shot to shame. I watch the ball sail until it dings against the farthest target. The screen above the clubs shows that she earned twelve points.

I give her a round of applause. "So this is why you wanted to come here?"

"I like the atmosphere," she says.

"Right."

"If you two are done eye-fucking," Darla sighs. "I'd appreciate some peace and quiet so I can concentrate."

"Darla!" Miley gasps.

The corner of Darla's mouth actually twitches up at Miley's outrage. "You're right. It's pointless to broadcast the obvious."

Darla sets up to take her next shot while I give Miley a long, *you seriously brought her,* kind of look. Miley at least has the decency to look like she regrets it now, if only just a little.

Despite Darla's constant drone of depressing, melodramatic one-liners, the night is one of the most fun I've had in a long time. Somewhere along the way, I forget I'm supposed to be proving my worth to Miley and I just enjoy spending time with her. But when Darla rolls her eyes at us for the hundredth time and says she's going to the bar to get drinks, Miley and I are alone for the first time since we got here.

I let out a long breath once Darla goes inside. "You feel that?" I ask.

"Feel what?" asks Miley.

"It's hard to say. Like a dark cloud just parted... like the sun is shining for the first--"

"Stop it!" laughs Miley, who swats at my arm. "Darla is really sweet once you get to know her."

"You'll have to pardon me if I find that hard to believe."

Miley smiles, picking at a loose chip of paint on the table. "I guess it's hard to go through what she and I went through together and not feel connected somehow, no matter how different we are. Some days I'd just excuse myself from class to go to the bathroom to be alone, and more often than not, Darla was already there. She laughs distantly. "We spent so much time talking about how much people suck in those bathrooms."

"Why did they tease you?" I ask, genuinely not understanding. From where I'm sitting, I see a beautiful woman. When she lets her guard down, her personality shines through so clearly it's like a beacon, and I can't wrap my head around what there would be not to like.

Her finger digs more forcefully at the chip of paint and her head tilts with the effort, lips pursing. "It depended on the year. When I was really little, it was my glasses--" she pauses at my confused look. "Contacts," she says, pointing to her eyes. "Then it was how bad I was at sports."

I nod, seeing something of a pattern. She got contacts because she was teased for her glasses. She practiced golf--and maybe other sports--because she was teased for not being any good.

"Then things really got ugly when the rumor started."

"The rumor?" I ask.

"I dated a guy in seventh grade named Jake, if you could even call it dating. He asked if I wanted to be his girlfriend, I said yes because I was stupid and lonely. He got his parents to take us to the movies and drop us off. I thought he was going to try to kiss me or hold my hand, but maybe he was too nervous, because we just watched the movie and that was it. It felt weird and awkward, so I broke things off with him the next day at school. That afternoon, I started noticing people acting weird around me. Girls were giving me dirty looks. Guys were leering at me and laughing. It was mortifying.

"It wasn't until Darla told me about the rumor going around that I knew why. She said Jake was telling everyone I gave him a blowjob during the movie and that I let him finger me. It didn't matter what really happened. All that mattered was the stupid lie he told because he wanted to save face."

I clench my teeth when I imagine her younger self dealing

with all that bullshit. "Let me guess, I'm not allowed to find this Jake asshole and punch him in the face?"

She smiles. "I'd rather you didn't."

"How did someone who went through so much hell end up so sweet?"

"Who says I'm sweet?" she asks with a devious little smirk.

I laugh. "Okay then, Miss Wild Thing. Tell me the worst thing you've ever done."

She leans forward, lowering her eyebrows dramatically. "Ninth grade. I was riding the bus on the way home from school and tossed my gum out the window without thinking. A second later, I heard a scream. I guess it went out my window and got sucked right back in a window near the back. It landed in Jenny Fisher's hair."

"Oh shit," I say, laughing.

"Yeah. And she went raging around the bus, screaming and threatening to get the principal involved if someone didn't fess up, but no one talked. I guess no one saw anything. And I didn't say a word. *And,*" she adds with a satisfied little smile. "I laughed my whole way home once I got off the bus, too. How's that for sweet?"

I grin. "That's it? That's your worst story?"

"What? You've got a better one?" she asks.

I tilt my head, mind immediately touching on some of the darker moments in my life--moments I don't care to bring to light right now. I haven't always been a good man, and I have the stories to prove it. There will be a time to share those stories with Miley, but our first real date isn't the right place, so I think back to when I was younger.

"Maybe," I say after dredging up an old memory. "I was a small kid back in middle school, and some of the other guys used to pick on me."

"Seriously?" asks Miley. "It's kind of hard to picture you having ever been small."

I chuckle. "Seriously. My older brother Leo was always big, though. So I knew most kids wouldn't take it too far when it came to bullying me. They all knew if any of it ever got back to my brother, he'd beat the shit out of them. But one day I got tired of it, of knowing my brother was the only thing standing between me and the other kids.

"So I made a plan. There was this hill the kids would ride their bikes down on the way home from school. It was a pretty steep road, but naturally, they liked to go as fast as they could. One afternoon, I hid on the side of the road in a bush with a bucket of loose gravel and rocks. I waited until I saw the kids who were always giving me shit at the top of the hill and gaining speed."

I pause, feeling a dark sort of guilt and ugliness rise up inside. I chose this story on a whim, only remembering it as the time I got those kids back--but in the telling of it, I'm realizing I was wrong for thinking some of the truly fucked up things I've done didn't reach back even to my childhood. My face twists a little as a finish the story.

"I threw the bucket of gravel out. I still remember the way their eyes bulged at me just before they hit the rocks. I could see so much in so few seconds: fear, regret, anger... Then all hell broke loose. The four of them went skidding and flipping down the hill. It must've been another ten feet to the bottom, and by the time they all got there, they were bloody and bruised, limping to their feet like they had just survived a bomb blast."

I laugh softly, but there's no humor in it. "They didn't even try to come after me. They just hobbled off, dragging their mangled bikes behind them. It was the last time anyone messed with me. The most fucked up part is I couldn't make myself feel bad for them. I just kept thinking to all the times they had tried to mess with me and what they would've done if they weren't afraid of my brother, and no matter how I looked at it, it felt like they got what they deserved."

I can imagine how it all must sound to Miley. She sees me now and probably can't imagine me back then, lanky and small, always trailing in my brother's shadow. If you looked at he and I side by side now, you'd never guess we were so different when we were kids. I caught up to him, but we took completely different paths to where we are today.

Instead of looking disgusted or appalled like I expect, Miley reaches across the table and squeezes my hand. The gesture surprises me--shocks me, even. I look down at her small hand on mine and know with more certainty than I felt before: she's the one. She's not just the perfect submissive for me, she's the perfect *woman*.

"I'm so sorry," she says. "You know the most messed up part?" she asks. "Somehow you have to feel like the bad guy when you stand up to the bullies. It doesn't really make sense, does it?"

I shake my head. "I think it's guilt. Guilt that there was probably another way to solve the problem without stooping to their level."

"Maybe. But should a dog feel guilty if it's backed into a corner and bites when it feels like it's run out of options?"

I grin. "You're really something, you know that?"

Her cheeks turn bright red and she looks away. A smile plays at her lips, but it seems like her shyness is winning the battle, because she smooths her features. "I don't know about that."

"I do," I say, taking her hand this time. "And I need to know this isn't the only date you're going to let me take you on."

"Hey," she says with mock anger. "The deal was that I get a whole date to decide."

I lean across the table inching closer to her. "I had something planned for the end of our date, but it's not going to work with her," I say, nodding toward Darla, who sits inside the building and is throwing back a glass of something brown.

"Then I guess it'll have to wait until date number two," says Miley.

I lick my lips. "You're a goddamn tease, do you know that?"

She aims her big, innocent baby blues eyes up at mine in the most irresistible way. "It'd only be teasing if you weren't going to get what you wanted."

"Then I get to pick the next date," I say.

She swallows, eyes still trained on mine as she regards me. "Deal."

7

MILEY

"You've got to talk to me sometime," Kyle says. He's yanking the laces on his shoes so hard it's a wonder they don't snap. "I was trying to protect you. That's all."

I cross my arms. It's not like I've been deliberately not talking to him, but after my date with Jayce last night, I came straight home and went to bed. "Protect me?" I ask. "You lied to him *and* me."

"I know.". He at least has the sense to look guilty, which wins him a few points. *But just a few.* "Look, it's just not the life I want for you. Hooking up with some BDSM club owner? What brother would want that for his sister."

"Did you you ever stop to think maybe what I want for myself is more important than what you want?"

He grimaces. "Of course it is. But look at your last few boyfriends. An alcoholic, a drug-addict, a guy who was secretly married, and a lowlife who bea--"

"I get it," I snap. "But this time feels different. I don't expect that to sound convincing or for you to believe me, but I can tell you this much. Every time you try to push us apart, some irrational, stubborn part of me is only going to want to get closer to him. So like it or not, you're going to just have to let this play out and see where it goes."

"What if where it goes is you getting hurt again?" he asks. "I can't just sit by while that happens."

"I can take care of myself, Kyle," I say more softly. He doesn't deserve my anger, not after everything he's done for me, so I push down all the negativity I might be feeling and make myself think back to all the times I've needed him and he's been there. "You've bailed me out of so many shitty situations, and I'm so thankful I have a big brother looking out for me. But you can't protect me forever. You've got to let me start figuring things out for myself, or I never will."

He lowers his head, resting his elbows on his knees as he sits on the couch, one shoe still untied. It's a long time before he looks back up and speaks. "I'll stay out of it as much as I can, but I swear to God. If he hurts you, I'll fucking kill him."

"Kyle..." I say.

"Fine, I'll just break his legs or something. Is that better?"

I laugh. "I guess that's fair."

Kyle grins. "Damn right it is." He laces up his shoe and gets up to give me a quick hug. "You'll tell me if you need my help, right?"

"Yes," I say. "Now get out of here. I've got plans today and I need to get ready."

He looks like he wants to say something--to ask what they are, but he impresses me when he ends up just nodding and leaving with a quick wave over his shoulder.

It's just a few minutes before Jayce is supposed to pick me up for our date tonight when my phone buzzes. I grab it off the counter and see I have a text from a number I don't recognize. I click to read it.

This isn't over. -Cade.

I set the phone down quickly on the counter. I blocked his number after we broke things off, so he either had to get a new phone or text me from someone else's to get that message through. For some reason, the extra effort makes it that much more ominous than if he had just drunk texted me. It makes me think he's completely sober, and still fuming over what happened when he tried to attack me in my apartment.

I make a quick call to block the new number, delete the text, and do my best to put it from my mind. As chilling as the threat was, I try to tell myself it's just his bruised ego talking. He probably wants to feel like he got the last word in and will now slink away like the snake he is.

I feel my stomach cramp in the oddest way, almost like I'm on my period even though it's not due for another week. I know it can't possibly be symptoms of a pregnancy yet, but my mind immediately goes to that night with Jayce. I got tested afterwards, but I'm still waiting on the results. As if that wasn't bad enough, I don't even know if my reckless night is going to lead to a baby.

I try to imagine Jayce's reaction if I am pregnant. There would be no doubt as to who the father is because Cade and I hadn't had sex in weeks before the break-up. He was content with beating me and forcing himself in my mouth to "shut" me up anytime I cried out. My bruises have faded to the point that I can cover them with makeup now, but I still feel the slight soreness every time I move. It's a shameful reminder of how bad I let things get, and it's also a wake up call about how careful I need to be with Jayce. I can't just let him charm me into complacency. I *won't* sit by and let things get out of hand again. Not that I can really imagine Jayce being like the men who came before him.

I feel like I got a glimpse inside that head of his last night at Galaxy Golf. I never would've thought a man like him could've had a childhood even remotely like mine, but he did, and he's more like me than I could have ever guessed. We've both suffered at the hands of others. We've both had our faces pressed to the ground and been told to give up, to quit. The difference is he overcame it. In so many ways, I still feel like there's a knee in my back, that constant force of oppression telling me I'm not good enough and I don't matter--saying I deserve all the things that have happened to me.

Knowing Jayce has been there and made it through what I have draws me to him more powerfully than any sexual attraction ever could--even if *that* part of my attraction to him is distractingly strong. I'd never admit as much to him, but submitting to Jayce was the most sublime, sensual experience of my life. Hardly an hour has gone by that I don't think back to a few nights ago and the way he claimed me in that cold, blue room while people watched.

A knock at the door startles me from my thoughts. I do a quick check of my hair in the hallway mirror and make sure my clothes and makeup still look okay before opening the door.

Jayce waits for me in a dark suit that manages to make his already broad shoulders look even more masculine. His hair is combed back in a way that somehow looks messy but neat and clean. It only takes one look in his eyes to know that his surprise date isn't going to be to a golf range.

"Evening," he says with a smoldering grin.

God. It's like I can forget how much of a presence he has in the time we're apart. A few minutes or a few hours and I start convincing myself he's not actually as consuming as I remember him being. I tell myself next time I'll be more composed around him, or that I'll have more self-control.

But whether he's letting his guard down and telling me about his past or commanding me to obey his every sexual desire, Jayce has a hold on me. I can't put my finger on why, but I feel it as surely as if there was a collar around my neck and a leash clutched firmly in his hand. Every moment I spend with him brings me closer to him--takes the slack out of the leash another few inches until I'm drawn so close I can feel the heat that practically burns from the surface of his skin.

Inch by inch, he's making me his, and every hour that goes by chips away at my desire to stop him.

"Hi," I say, my voice feeling thick and awkward.

He smoothly takes my arm and leads me into the hall, where he closes my door and waits for me to lock it. "I see they fixed it," he says, nodding to the door he smashed down when he burst into stop Cade.

"Yeah," I say. "Thank you, by the way. I would've gotten it handled if you hadn't sent over that repair guy."

"You break it, you buy it," he says with a casual wave of his hand. "Besides, I liked having an excuse to do something nice for you. I think most women would've already dropped about two thousand hints for me to buy them something ridiculously expensive. You hardly seem to care."

"We never had much," I say as we wait for the elevator. "Growing up, I mean. My dad worked a factory job trying to make enough to support us on his own, but he probably spent half of it on booze, so... our Christmas tree and our pantry were always pretty barren."

The elevator dings. Jayce guides me inside by the small of my back. Something in his touch is so reassuring. It's protective--possessive, even--but it doesn't make me feel claustrophobic like my brother's over-protectiveness. It makes me feel safe and secure. *Happy.*

"I'd think that would make you even more interested in money," he says.

"I guess it could've. But if I had learned to rely on money for happiness, I would've had a really hard time ever being happy. So maybe I just forced myself to stop thinking about it."

"Have you been happy?" he asks. The tone of his voice is so gentle that his question touches me in a way I wouldn't think just a few words could.

I feel my throat get tight and tears sting at my eyes, but I master my emotions with a brief struggle and force out the words. "Sometimes. Maybe." It's the truth. I could've said yes. I could've lied to him, but there was so much compassion in the way he asked, that I couldn't bring myself to lie to him.

"That's going to change," he says firmly. "When you're mine."

His words send a trickle of heat through my body that pools in my stomach and makes my breath feel short. "You mean as a submissive?" I ask.

"I mean mine," he says.

I wait for him to elaborate, but he apparently thinks he's made his point and stands quietly until the elevator reaches the ground floor.

JAYCE PARKS HIS CAR OUTSIDE HIS CLUB, LOOKING OVER TO ME IN A very serious--*very sexy*--way. "You had your turn taking me on the date you wanted. I played along nicely, didn't I?"

"Yes..." I say slowly, not liking where this is going.

"Now it's your turn to play nicely for me. Though I hope you'll end up doing more than just playing," he adds with a hint of a smirk. "I want you to be my submissive for the night. Not just in private. Not in some dark room where no one can see you. I want to show you off."

I swallow. "In there?" I ask.

He nods. "And I want you to wear these while I do," he says, his smirk widening as he lifts a pair of black panties from within the center console.

I frown at them, even though the idea of wearing the panties *he* wants me to wear already has heat building between my legs. "Why those?" I ask.

He waggles a finger at me. "No more questions, princess. If you're going to learn how to truly please me as a submissive, it's time you start learning how to properly behave. So you *will* put these panties on, and you'll let me watch."

"What?" I ask.

His expression darkens.

It only takes a look to make it perfectly clear to me that I'm not supposed to be asking questions or trying to get any kind of explanation. I'm just supposed to obey. There's a freedom in the realization, a kind of reckless abandon in what he's promising, and despite all my reservations, doubts, and fears from the past, I know I want to say yes.

I watch him with a defiant look as I shimmy out of my panties, careful to keep my dress from riding up and giving him *too* good of a view as I do. To my surprise, he holds out his hands like he expects me to hand him the panties. I do as he wants, which makes another rush of excited heat flood my body. *God.* He's so confident. There's not a hint of shame or embarrassment over wanting to take my used panties, and while the kinky request might creep me out coming from anyone else, the unapologetic confidence Jayce has makes it far from creepy. Somehow he makes it sexy, even.

I take the black panties and slide into them, noticing that Jayce doesn't even try to hide the fact that he's watching my every move.

"Perfect," he says once I've got them on. "Now we can begin."

He gets out of the car, opens my door, and helps me up. "There are a few rules you will need to follow, or you'll find out why you're wearing those panties."

I frown in confusion, but he continues on, ignoring my unasked question.

"First, you will not make eye contact with another man so long as we are in the club. Second, you will not speak unless spoken to. Third, you will obey me without question, no matter what my request. Lastly, you give me the respect I deserve as your Dom and refer to me as Sir. Do you have any questions?"

Only a few thousand. "No. *Sir,*" I say, nearly forgetting to call him Sir already.

The club bustles with activity, as usual, but for the first time I feel like one of the sexy women I watch slink around with handsome men, watching from my side of the bar longingly at something I could never have. It feels good to be possessed by Jayce. He makes it painfully clear to anyone who looks our way that I'm his by holding his hand in the center of my back and subtly guiding me as he moves, making sure I stay perfectly in step with him.

I scan the crowd for Cade because his threatening text is still fresh in my mind. I don't know if I ever really got to know the real Cade during the unfortunate time I spent dating him, but I do know that men like him don't just walk away. Especially, not after what happened with Jayce in my apartment. Still, standing beside Jayce, I know I'm safe. At least from other men. I guess the jury is still out on whether I'm safe from him.

I have to do a very un-ladylike step as I try to discreetly spread my legs a little to adjust the panties Jayce has me wearing. They feel slightly odd near the front, like the material is thicker or they are heavier than usual, but my subtle move seems to relieve the discomfort.

It seems like Jayce knows every single person in the club. I lose track of how many people he introduces me to, and each time he specifically explains that I'm his submissive. I can't say why, but no matter how many couples he tells I'm his submissive, I feel proud every time. Maybe it's just the simple fact that Jayce is jaw-droppingly gorgeous, and I'd have to be out of my mind *not* to be proud to have him walking around practically bragging about having me.

As far as I can tell, I obey all of Jayce's rules, until a man and two women stop us just as Jayce seems to be leading us to one of the back areas of the club.

"Jayce Carlyle in the flesh!" says the man in a booming voice.

I carefully avoid looking up to see his face. Even though Jayce doesn't seem to be looking my way as he greets the trio, I feel like he'll know if I break his rule somehow. All I can see is that the man is barrel-chested and almost bursts out of the expensive suit he wears. The women at his side are full of thick, beautiful curves, but just to be on the cautious side, I don't look up and meet their eyes, either.

"Barry," says Jayce in a neutral tone that tells me he isn't a particularly big fan of this man. "It's good to see you and your new..."

"These two are just run-of-the-mill submissives," explains Barry, who gives both women a generous squeeze on their asses as if punctuating his point. "No slaves for me this season. Too complicated. Too many rules and too much commitment. Am I right?"

"I wouldn't know," Jayce says dryly.

Barry's feet shift, and though I'm staring down at his shoes, I can tell he's facing me now. "And who is this lovely minx at your side?"

"This is Miley, my submissive."

"Ahhh, is she now? Does she speak?" he asks with a falsely playful tone.

"Not to you," Jayce says. His tone has gone from neutral to cold.

Barry snaps his fingers, which draws my eyes instinctively up--where I accidentally look straight into his eyes. He has thick eyebrows and mediterranean features, but there's something cocky and dirty in his expression I don't like at all.

I look immediately back to the ground, but I see Jayce reach a hand into his pocket and I nearly gasp out loud when my pussy starts to *vibrate*. My eyes go wide and I move my hands half-way toward my crotch to suppress the vibrations before I realize how crazy I would look. I'm forced to keep my hands at my side and close my eyes, slowly piecing together what's going on.

The panties...

He made me wear some kind of panties with a remote-controlled vibrator, and he must have the remote in his pocket. So my punishment is to have to endure the maddeningly good sensation in public--just a few inches away from people.. I put a hand to my mouth as carefully as I can, acting like I'm coughing to disguise the hitching of breath that drew their eyes.

I see Jayce grinning when no one else is looking, and I tell myself I need to find a way to pay him back for this particular cruel creativity if I ever get the chance.

"Are you alright, dear?" asks Barry, who steps forward and starts to reach for me.

Jayce steps between us, knocking Barry's hand away so quickly I barely see it happen. "You'll keep your eyes and your hands off my submissive if you want to remain welcome in my club. Am I making myself clear?"

Barry stutters out an apology, laughing awkwardly as he does. "Of course, of course, Mr. Carlyle. I was only trying to help, I do hope you'll find it in your heart to..." he says, trailing off when Jayce leads me away from the man before he's even finished apologizing.

It's only once we start walking that Jayce finally turns off the vibrations. He leads me into one of the back rooms, pausing to look at me before we move in. "Each time you break one of my rules, I'll leave it on longer. And don't think I won't make you cum in public, princess, because I'm just waiting for you to give me an excuse."

I frown. "He wasn't supposed to even look at me, but you're okay with me cumming in front of strangers?"

Jayce pulls a small black object out of his pants and presses the button, setting the vibrations off. I clutch the hem of my dress from the intensity of the vibrations, which seem even more powerful than the first time.

The sensation takes the breath from my lungs, and Jayce

moves me until my back is against the door frame and his body is inches from mine. "I'm answering you only because I choose to, princess. But you will pay the consequences for questioning me each and every time you dare to."

I nod my head and close my eyes. My body is already shaking from the tremors of pleasure running through me like tendrils of flame. It's not just the vibrations. It's the exposure, the strangeness of being in plain sight of anyone who cared enough to look. All the elements blend together into a wonderful mix of euphoria tinged with the fear that I will start moaning and making a scene by having an orgasm in the middle of the crowded club for seemingly no reason.

"I can't tolerate a man like him touching you or even thinking of you. But with a certain level of anonymity and detachment, I *would* enjoy taking you in public."

I want to tell him how confusing that is and how little sense it makes, but if I'm being honest with myself I can understand to a certain degree. There is a strong vibe of creepiness coming from Barry. So I understand how him looking at me sexually or trying to touch me would seem more personal and intimdate, even if it was only one-sided. But being taken by Jayce in front of others, like that first night in the room with the glass window... that felt different. It was just something thrilling and exciting in the background.He clicks the button, stopping the vibrations, but not immediately stepping away from me. "The intensity will keep going up," he says. "So if you think you'll be able to keep avoiding a scene when you misbehave, you may want to reconsider."

He takes me by the small of my back again, finally leading me through the doorway into one of the areas set off from the main lobby. I still haven't been inside any of these areas except the room with the stage I saw that first night Jayce took me, and the blue room.

I'm completely shocked when I realize we're in a restaurant. I thought I had smelled food a couple of times before when I was behind the bar, but I always thought I imagined it because the smell was so faint. The idea that an entire kitchen and wait staff works here and I had no idea is more than a little surprising. Booths and tables are arranged much like they would be at a dinner show, except the *show* on the stage is seven bare-chested men and one completely naked woman.

I stop, looking toward the scene in a mixture of horror and fascination. She's bound by ropes that suspend her from the ceiling and blindfolded. The skin of her breasts and ass is pink, and my guess it's from the paddles some of the men are holding. "Jayce!" I whisper in alarm. "Is she okay?"

"I'm going to forgive the fact that you spoke out of turn, because your concern here is reasonable. But yes, she's probably having the most sensually enlightening moment of her life right now. She volunteered for this, after all. In fact, the waitlist to be featured like this is so long she likely had to wait several weeks for her turn."

"She wanted this?" I ask incredulously.

"This lifestyle has many, *many* things to offer for many different appetites, princess."

"Does that kind of thing turn you on?" I ask, feeling a little nervous for the answer. I'm not about to judge him for his sexual fantasies, but at the same time, I'm desperately hoping he wouldn't ever want me to do something like that, because I know I couldn't. I wouldn't want him to be okay with sharing me with that many men, either--or *any* men, for that matter.

"Personally? No," he says. "I've never been particularly drawn to the extremes of BDSM. It has never been about extremes for me. Think of it like this: everyone has a line. For some, the line is drawn before their clothes even come off. For others, the line is sex with a stranger,, or with ten strangers. The most important thing is to find your line and bring yourself to the absolute edge of it. You'll never feel greater pleasure than when you're strad-dling the line between too much and not enough. Go over the line, and your discomfort will taint your pleasure. Stay too far away from it and you're cheating the experience."

"Where's your line?" I ask.

"That's the thing," he says with a grin. "One of the reasons I know you're meant to be my submissive is that I feel something I've never felt before when I'm with you. I feel like my line is irrelevant now. My line is wherever yours is. Your limit is my own, and nothing will bring me greater pleasure than to help you find that edge again and again, because it will continually move as we explore.I want to be there with you as it does so we can find it together."

I laugh a little awkwardly, not quite knowing what to say. "I've only known you a few days," I say. "You're talking like we're going to be together forever."

Even as I say them, my words sound harsh and colder than I intended. I know it's a defense mechanism--a wall I'm putting up because I'm still afraid he's going to hurt me if I let him in too close. I hate myself for it. Jayce has been nothing but good to me, and he's the first guy who is actually making an effort to get to know the real me, yet I can't seem to stop subconsciously pushing him away.

Somehow, Jayce manages to take my words in stride. He doesn't even seem annoyed when he answers. "What would be the point of dating you if I didn't plan on forever?"

I open my mouth to respond, but close it again before I say something stupid.

He puts both hands to my cheeks, rubbing my lips with his thumb in a longing sort of way that makes me tingle all over. "I know you have been through a lot, and I won't even try to pretend I can understand what it was like. But I can promise you this much. Let me, and I'll take care of you. I'll treat you the way you deserve to be treated. I'll care about you more than you ever imagined someone could. I swear it."

For some reason, tears well up in my eyes, but I manage to

blink them away quickly, hopefully before he sees. There's so much I want to say to him right now, but all I can manage is a quiet "thank you."

He kisses my forehead. "Come on," he says gently, but still manages to infuse the words with enough command that I might as well be pulled by a leash as he walks. "And no more free passes," he says with a grin. "Break the rules again and you'll pay."

"Yes, sir."

I expect him to take us to an empty booth, but instead, he has us sit with a couple who might be in their mid sixties near the back. I nearly give Jayce a confused look, but worry he might consider that questioning him--so I keep my eyes down as we sit. I can't say why, but every time I have to force myself to obey his rules and conform to the image he expects for his submissive, I feel a rush of satisfaction. Just knowing I'm pleasing him and being what he wants makes me feel more desirable than I've ever felt in my life, and as sad as it is, I can't seem to get enough of his small looks of approval when I follow his rules. I hardly want to think of my father at a time like this, but his way was to ask for perfection. When he got it, there wasn't so much as a sniff of approval, and when we fell short of what he wanted, there was hell to pay.

So this world Jayce is letting me play a part in feels *right*. The rules are clear, the punishments are swift and so far, enticing in a dirty way. They stretch the limits of my comfort, but not so far as to make me fearful, especially when every time I do what I'm supposed to, I can tell it's making Jayce happy.

"Mr. Carlyle," the man says. I can tell he probably broke a lot of hearts when he was younger, and his companion is no different. I realize I was looking at his face and quickly avert my eyes to the woman at his side, hoping Jayce didn't notice my slip of concentration. Her lips are curved in a catlike grin while she watches us, gorgeous blue eyes appraising and hard.

"I wanted to introduce you to my submissive," Jayce says.

"And I thought she might be interested to meet the club's most experienced dominant and submissive."

"You mean *oldest?*" asks the man with a grin. "I'm Dennis," he says to me. "And this is Catrina."

Jayce chuckles. "Old or experienced. Call it what you will, I was hoping you could explain the history of the club to her. I know you were around long before I ever purchased it and I think she could learn a great deal from you."

Dennis makes a pleased sound that strikes a note of nervousness in me. If I know one thing about *experienced* men, it's that history seems to be an inexhaustible point on which they can talk about for ages.

I'm thoroughly confused now, as I can't see any reason Jayce would want me to have a history lesson on the club, but Dennis begins in earnest, starting with when the building was constructed and how he was actually there at the construction site.

It's only a few seconds before Jayce's hand slides across my thigh under the table. Between trying not to make eye contact with the man who is telling me a story and trying not to look suspicious as Jayce lifts my dress, I feel more than a little tense.

He starts to rub against my panties, sending chills through me and making my already wet pussy throb.

Dennis doesn't seem to notice, though it's hard to tell when all I can look at are his wildly gesturing hands. But when I sneak a glance up at Catrina, she's watching with me a great deal of interest and an even wider grin than before, unless I'm imagining it.

Jayce's hand slips inside my panties, sliding through my wet folds effortlessly.

I squirm, trying not to close my eyes or moan as he starts to alternate between circling my clit and plunging his fingers inside me. I lean my elbow on the table and put a hand to my mouth, trying to cover the sound of what are now little gasps that I can't seem to control.

Somewhere through the haze of pleasure, I realize Jayce brought us to this particular table precisely so he could get Dennis rambling while he finger-fucked me just a few feet away from two strangers. *Bastard.* But as dirty as it is, being pleasured like this without either of them knowing is absolutely thrilling. I press my thighs together, trying to control the shaking that wants to rip through my body, but the pressure only buries Jayce's fingers deeper inside me.

I sneak a look to the side, wondering how obvious what he's doing is from the movement of his arm, but I'm impressed to see he's somehow keeping it completely still. Only his wrist, hand, and fingers are moving, all of which are below the table.

"...And wouldn't you believe it?" asks Dennis, who looks to Catrina as he pauses for dramatic effect. "They knew where the plans were the whole time!" he announces, banging his hand on the table as he breaks into a bout of laughter.

A moan slips out of my mouth, and I'm thankful for the timing, because I force it to turn into a series of gasping, very strange laughs. Catrina covers her mouth, eyes lit with amusement as she watches me. She knows what's going on. I can feel it.

My cheeks burn so hot I think I might actually be giving off my own light source.

Jayce is relentless though, and he keeps working magic with his fingers, not caring how much more obvious it's becoming by the second that something is going on.

I try to look anywhere but at the people who must surely be starting to suspect something, and make the mistake of looking toward the stage. The woman is riding one man while another crouches behind her to fuck her in the ass, and she has her mouth around a third man's cock while she works two more still with her hands. It's so perverted and completely wrong, but at this particular moment, I'm not exactly thinking with my conservative side, and it's just enough to push me over the edge.

My hand comes down hard enough on the table to make Dennis and Catarina's drink glasses rattle. I look up, even as the orgasm is spearing through me and making my eyes want to shut. "That was incredible," I breathe with far too much enthusiasm than the boring story warranted. "I can't believe..." I say, sucking in air. "This place has so much history."

Dennis, who somehow appears completely oblivious, nods enthusiastically. "If more young folks like you showed an interest in the history around here, I think the world would be a much better place."

"It's true," Catarina agrees with a knowing smile. "He says it all the time."

Jayce slides his hand out of my panties and to my sheer disbelief, brings his fingers up to his mouth where he *licks them clean.* Oh my God. I watch him, biting my lip and completely oblivious to how Dennis and Catarina must be looking at us.

"Can I be excused for a moment? I need to use the ladies room," I say. The real reason is I feel so flushed and strange being this wet in public, I want to make sure I'm not getting anything on my dress. That, and I need a mental breather from Jayce before he pulls any more crazy stunts.

Jayce narrows his eyes at me, clearly disappointed. "I have to pee," I whisper, hoping that's enough of an excuse for him not to use the vibrator on me again.

My panties buzz just for a split second, making me falter as I'm walking away from the table. I turn to look back at Jayce when the vibration stops almost immediately. He winks at me and then grins.

I give him a playful glare before heading toward a waiter and asking where the restrooms are. I walk into a small hall off to the side of the main room just as someone bumps into me, nearly knocking me back.

I start to apologize, my words fall short when I see who I knocked into. "Cade?" I ask. I take a step back, sucking in a breath to yell for Jayce, but Cade pulls me into a darkened corner of the hallway and pins me to the wall, pressing his hand to my mouth so I can't scream.

"Scream and I'll make you regret it," he says, bulging his eyes at me until I nod my head.

He pulls his hand away and I suck in a breath to scream, but he slams his hand back against my mouth, bashing my head into the wall as he does. I wince as the impact gives me an immediate headache.

"God, it's easy to forget what a fucking bitch you are," he says. "But I'll pretend none of this happened. All you have to do is come back to me, baby. You think he's a dom? Fuck him. I can be the best dom you've ever had in your life."

I try to pull his hands away and kick at him, but he uses his knees to pin my legs against the wall and slaps away my hands with his free hand effortlessly. "Go ahead and cry to your new boyfriend. Tell him I hurt you. That's all you were ever good at. Fucking crying. And when he doesn't do shit about it, you can come back to me when you realize you need a real man."

He shoves me to the side, knocking me down to my knees, where I stay for a few seconds, gasping for breath and wiping the feel of his hand from my face. I want to scream, but all the conditioning from my past rises up in me. The same conditioning that made me weak and kept me from doing anything when guys would treat me like shit. That weakness kept me coming back like a silly, stupid little girl until it got so bad they practically broke me before it got through my blindness.

I shouldn't be surprised that my instinct is to stay quiet and bottle it up, though. My dad started training me there was no use fighting back or telling anyone from a young age. I can still remember how I told a family friend about what my dad had been doing to us after one of his bad spells. Instead of telling the cops, they told my dad I had been telling stories, and I swear he nearly killed me that night.

I slowly get to my feet, just before a woman comes around the corner and gives me a concerned look, but doesn't stop before entering the bathroom. I wait a few seconds for my head to stop spinning and step inside after her. I check the damage in the mirror, which isn't as bad as I thought, and make my way back to Jayce, who is talking with Dennis about some kind of business deal they apparently were in on together a few years ago.

I give him a tight smile that I hope looks genuine as I sit, keeping my eyes down.

Jayce stops mid-sentence. "I'm sorry," he says, holding a hand up to Dennis and Catarina. "Would you excuse us?"

"Of course," says Dennis.

Jayce leads me away from the room with the stage into a quieter room, where slow jazz plays and men and women lounge on leather couches, some kissing or fondling, but most just cuddling. Purple light bathes everything, from the people to the glasses of wine and champagne set out for members on several tables throughout the room.

Jayce keeps walking me through the room without saying a word until he takes me to one of a dozen booths set into the wall. He pulls the curtain closed, which offers us complete privacy. For a moment, we're in total darkness, until he lights a match and ignites the candle at the center of the table.

I want to ask what's going on, but I know he'll tell me when he's ready, so I keep my mouth closed and wait.

"I need you to tell me what happened," he says stonily.

I reel back, taken off guard. "What happened?" I ask stupidly.

He leans forward until his gorgeous face is lit in flickering orange light. "You left. You came back. Something happened in between."

I open my mouth wordlessly, trying and failing to think of

how I can explain why I didn't say anything to him when I came back.

"I need to know," he growls. "Something happened to my princess, and I want to fucking know what it was so I know whose ass to kick."

I shake my head, letting out a frustrated sigh. "Maybe I didn't tell you because I don't just want somebody kicking anyone's ass who treats me wrong."

"So someone did something to you?" he asks, bull headedly ignoring the point I'm trying to make.

I clutch my temples, letting my head fall. "I don't know what's wrong with me, okay? I just don't ever seem to do the right thing when guys are involved. I always let them hurt me and make me feel like shit. It's only after it's over that I realize what I should've done," I say, blurting out more than I intended. "Maybe my instincts are just crap."

Jayce is clearly trying to control his anger, so his words come out clipped and forced. "I can't help if I don't know what happened."

"Cade was here," I say, looking up. "Okay? He..." my lips curl with disgust when I think about how I let him do that to me and just walk away--how I wasn't even going to say anything. "He was here," is all I can manage.

Jayce's nostrils flare and his hands clench into fists. "That shouldn't be possible. I had all the security personally shown his picture and told not to let him in under any circumstances."

"Apparently it was."

8

JAYCE

I look across the candle-lit table to Miley, who looks so fucking perfect with the soft orange light illuminating her features. The idea of that fucking scumbag so much as talking to her has my blood boiling. I'm ready to go rampage through the club, shaking down my bouncers and staff until I find which incompetent idiot was responsible for letting him into the club. One thing's for sure though, if I thought I was going overboard in my preparations to keep him out of here before, I'm about to set a new fucking bar.

"Wait here," I say, starting to slide out of the booth to stand.

Miley's arm snaps across the table, gripping my wrist. "Please," she says in the smallest, most fragile voice. "Please don't go."

I sit back down, fighting every instinct in my body that has me ready to rip Cade's head off. "I might still be able to catch him."

"And then what?" she asks.

"Then I'll teach him what happens when he comes near you," I say.

"Like last time? You could've killed him in my apartment, and he still came back. Jayce... Kyle has been acting like an enforcer for me my whole life. Once a guy mistreats me, he shows up and kicks his ass. You know how much that has helped me avoid getting treated like shit from the next guy that comes along? None."

"So I'm just supposed to sit by while this ex keeps showing up and harassing you? Fuck that."

"No," she says, pinching the bridge of her nose and hesitating a long time before she speaks again. "My dad never treated me right... not even close. And every time I tried to fight back it only got worse. So I learned a long time ago the best way to make it stop is just... play dead."

I shake my head. "No," he says. "I refuse to accept that. You don't deserve to have to cower when this fucker comes around. You deserve to be free of that shit, and so help me God, if he makes the mistake of showing his face when I'm around, he's done."

"It's not about whether you accept it or not," she snaps. "It's about what I want."

My lips twitch at the sound of her raising her voice to me. "Be careful how you talk to me," I warn.

"Or what?" she asks defiantly. "Are you going to hit me too? Slap me around? Show your true colors?"

I grit my teeth. "Don't," I say.

"Don't what? Don't make you mad, because then I'll see what kind of man you really are?"

"No," I say, forcing myself to calm down. "Don't push me away when you need me most."

She makes an annoyed sound and gets up like she's about to leave. I get out of my side of the booth and cut her off, forcing her back into the booth. She struggles against me briefly, swinging her hands wildly and trying to free herself, but I pull her in tight, forcing her to accept my embrace as I hug her to my chest. "Don't push me away," I whisper, stroking her back as her hands slowly wrap around my back and she digs her fingers into me, shaking with sobs. "Let me look out for you, princess. I'll keep you safe. I'll protect you."

AFTER I'VE DROPPED MILEY BACK OFF AT HER APARTMENT FOR THE night, I decide to do a little research. I know she wanted me to let it be, but I also know I won't be able to sleep as long as this fucker is out there, just looking for his chance to harass her again.

Finding his address isn't hard, because all members of the club have to submit payment information, including their billing address. He lives about five blocks from Miley, which is about a thousand blocks too close for my liking. I park outside his place, straighten my jacket, and walk into the lobby of the apartment complex. It's a nice place, and probably costs almost twenty grand a month, if my guess is any good.

His apartment is on the second floor, last one at the end of the hall. I knock a few times and wait. I want nothing more than to deck him again, maybe harder this time so he doesn't get back up, but that's not what I came here for.

When the door swings open, Cade is squinting at me through bleary, drunken eyes. His hair is a mess and his tie is halfway undone and his shirt is untucked. From the looks of it, he came straight home to drown himself in some booze after he fucked with Miley at the club.

"Mind if I come in?" I ask stonily.

He makes a dismissive sound and tries to slam the door, but I plant a firm palm on the door, holding it open, even as he struggles to force it closed. He eventually realizes it's useless and sighs dramatically. "The fuck do you want from me? Wanna know how she liked it in the sack? Or maybe--"

"It would be smart if you stopped there," I say through clenched teeth. "I told myself I wasn't going to fuck you up tonight, but I only have so much patience, asshole."

Cade considers me, probably replaying the moment that left

him with the swollen nose and dark bruise he still wears on his face. "*What?*" he asks petulantly.

"I'm giving you one last warning. If it was up to me, your warning would be the beating I want to give you, but you're getting a warning instead."

He raises his eyebrows. "That's supposed to scare me?"

"No, dumbass," I say. "It's supposed to make it painfully obvious that you need to fuck off." I lean forward so I'm close enough to smell the stink of his breath. "If I hear about you harassing Miley again, I'll come back, and it's not going to be for a warning. Understand me?"

He licks his lips, taking me in from head to toe, as if he's trying to decide if he really should take my threat seriously. "Whatever, man. She's not worth my time anyway."

He slams the door on me.

I let out a long breath. *Fuck.* Not hitting him might have been the single greatest act of love in the history of mankind, because if I wasn't sure I was falling for Miley, I would've killed that asshole. But every time I think about her my pulse races and I can't get my mind off the next time I'll see her and the things I can't wait to do to her.

I already know exactly what I'm doing to her tomorrow night, though, whether she does or not. I'm taking her to a party at my house, but she's not going to see much of the party. I'll be too excited to show her the surprise I have waiting upstairs.

9

MILEY

"Wow," I say.

Jayce pulls his car to a stop at the top of a relatively steep hill, where a sprawling mansion sits. The huge, circular driveway is choked with luxury cars and glamorous couples who look filthy rich even from a distance. Every woman glimmers with ridiculously huge diamond jewelry and designer dresses. The men are distinguished, young, rugged, handsome, and just about every combination of attractive I could imagine. It makes me realize just how unbelievably hot Jayce is though, because even these men can't compete with him.

I wait in my seat as he walks around to the passenger side and gets the door for me. When he takes my hand and helps me out, I feel like a princess being escorted to a ball by a ruggedly handsome prince.

"Do you like it?" he asks. He tosses his keys to a valet who hops in and goes to move the car out of the main driveway.

"The party?" I ask.

"The house," he says.

"Oh. Yes. It's breathtaking."

He nods. "It's one of my favorite properties, though my little cabin in the woods still blows it out of the water."

I can't help bulging my eyes a little at him. "This is *your* house? I know your club is nice, but I didn't think--"

He chuckles. "I've been fortunate. Some good investments, some wild risks... You'd be surprised how fast it can add up. You know the strange thing?" he asks. "You spend all this time thinking it'll feel a certain way, like if you only had enough money, *then* you could really be happy. But all the money I made only made me feel lonelier." He shakes his head, laughing a little at himself. "Pretty pathetic, I guess. I throw these crazy parties just so I don't have to come home to a huge, empty reminder of how far I've come but how little it means."

"I can't imagine you being lonely," I say carefully. "I mean, a guy like you doesn't exactly fly under the radar, especially not to women. There's probably not a woman in the entire city who wouldn't kill to have a night with you." I hate what I'm doing, but I can't stop myself. Even though I believe what I'm saying, some insecure part of me is wanting him to tell me otherwise. I want to know he's not a playboy who is fast and loose with relationships, that I'm not just the next target in a long line of conquests for him.

"Even if that were true," he says as we walk together toward the main entrance. "If someone tried to give you ten thousand spoons and all you needed was a knife, you'd still have a problem."

I stop dead in my tracks, looking at him in disbelief. "Did you just use a quote from an Alanis Morissette song un-ironically?"

"No," he says, failing to hold back a smirk. "I think it *was* ironic."

I clap a hand to my forehead, bursting with laughter. "Oh my God. Please tell me you didn't just set me up for that on purpose."

"I wouldn't lie to you," he says.

I shake my head in disbelief. "Are you sure you don't have kids from a previous relationship? Because that was dangerously close to a dad joke."

He grins, but it's half-hearted. "No. I'm not interested in having kids."

"I see," I say, clearing my throat. A thick silence hangs between us as we walk inside and are bombarded with loud music and the sight of hundreds of people dancing, laughing, talking, and drinking.

My stomach decides to send another nervous cramp my way right at that moment, as if to remind me that I could possibly be carrying his baby. I would've thought with everything he has said to me that the idea of a baby would actually excite him. A silly part of me was even starting to fantasize about what it would be like if I really was carrying his child. How it would force me to overcome my fear that I'm destined to pick the wrong guy, because a baby would take the choice out of my hands--like the cosmos putting a big neon arrow over his head *for* me. Now my fantasy seems more like a nightmare. At best he'd want nothing to do with it. At worst, there's the possibility that he might try to talk me into an abortion, which I would never agree to.

Even if I'm not pregnant, that single statement feels like it cuts through me to my foundation: *He doesn't want kids.* If I really decide he's the right guy, it would mean I could never have the family I've always wanted.

I'm about to ask him more when a tall, strikingly handsome man and a beautiful woman approach us at the door. The man holds a glass of amber liquor casually as he approaches, and the woman at his side wears an eye-catching necklace with a loop, almost like a collar.

"Jayce!" says the man warmly. "Thank God you finally cut off that man-bun. I like this better," he says, reaching for Jayce's hair, but Jayce slaps his hand away with a grin.

"Miley," says Jayce. "This is my brother, Leo, and his wife, Lysa."

"It's nice to meet you I say," reaching to shake their hands. Now that he says it, I can see the family resemblance in Leo. I can also picture this mountain of a man intimidating Jayce's would-be bullies when they were younger.

"Be careful with this family," says Lysa, who shakes my hand and flashes me an open, friendly smile. "They'll suck you in and never let go."

Leo pulls her closer, as if to confirm her statement. She grins up at him. The way she looks at him makes my heart melt. I've seen so many couples who act like strangers, enemies, or maybe the worst--like business partners. The way they look at each other erases any possibility of that. I feel a deep longing to have that kind of bond with someone, too.

I'm not kidding myself, though. Right now, I have a deep longing to have that kind of bond with a very particular some-one--a someone who makes terrible dad jokes, has a soft side, and shows a command over my body like nothing I ever could've imagined. *Someone who doesn't want kids.*

"Is that such a bad thing?" Jayce asks. His fingers splay across my back and he pulls me just a little closer.

"Maybe if it's you doing the pulling," Leo says with a grin.

Jayce tenses. "Don't make me show off to my girlfriend by kicking your ass."

"Like the last time you tried? I think I remember that ending with me holding you in a headlock."

Jayce grins. "You were still trying to woo Lysa. I just didn't want to embarrass you. I could've flipped you at least three times."

"Oh?" Leo laughs, stripping off his jacket and tossing it on a nearby chair.

Jayce takes his own off and sets his jacket aside.

I frown in confusion as the two men squat into athletic poses, hands out wide like they are about to wrestle.

Lysa nods for me to come with her toward the bar. I follow her, glancing back over my shoulder as Jayce and Leo collide and start grunting, taking turns trying to flip each other to the ground while a handful of people gather to watch and cheer them on.

"It's part of the package," Lysa shrugs. "Unfortunately, if you want to land yourself a guy like one of the Carlyles, you have to deal with occasional bouts of over-the-top masculine displays."

There's a loud cheer as Jayce manages to pin Leo on his back and starts trying to get some kind of grip on Leo's arm.

"You sure this is normal?" I ask, unable to stop watching the spectacle.

"These two wrestled like monkeys the first time Leo brought me to a party, too. I think it's just how they bond. Maybe in their minds it's like a macho handshake."

Jayce pulls his arm back like he's about to punch Leo while he sits on his stomach, but Leo twists at the last second, using his hips to throw Jayce to the ground and climb on top of him.

I flinch back. "Oh my God. They're going to kill each other."

"They'll be fine. Look. I saw the way Jayce was watching you. He's serious about you, you know. Guys can't fake that look."

"You were probably just imagining it," I say. "We've only known each other a couple days."

Lysa's smile broadens. "You'd be surprised what kind of feelings can form in a couple days."

"Was it like that with you and Leo?"

Lysa makes an amused face. "Something like that, yeah."

The small crowd groans in disappointment, drawing my eyes back to the fight. Jayce and Leo are dusting each other off and laughing about something as they walk toward us.

"Who won?" Lysa asks.

Both men point to themselves at the same time, drawing a laugh from Lysa and I.

"Well, as good as it is to see you," Jayce says to Leo, "I want to give Miley the grand tour of the upstairs."

Leo and Lysa exchange a knowing look that makes me equal parts nervous and excited. I blush, waving goodbye to them sheepishly before Jayce drags me away.

"Do you seriously just brawl with him every time you guys run into each other?" I ask.

Jayce scoffs. "No. Maybe half of the time at most. We're not barbarians," he adds with no hint of self-awareness.

I smile to myself, clinging a little tighter to his arm. The side of Jayce I met that first night in the club was all sexuality. Every movement, action, and word seemed to resonate with my pulse, driving me closer and closer to some kind of uncontrollable frenzy. I had trouble picturing anything else from him. I couldn't imagine what breakfast would've been like--I mean, was he going to just pounce across the table and screw me whenever the need rose up? Would we be able to talk about our day? Watch a show together in the evening?

I didn't know, but I thought I did. Now I've seen there's more to him. *Yes*, the sexual energy is never far below the surface, but ever since he told me about his childhood it feels like I have this kind of connection that goes deeper than the night we shared. He understands my past because he lived his own version of it.

Maybe I never realized how important that was because I was always dating the bully, not the bullied. Even though I doubt anyone would be dumb enough to try to bully Jayce *now*, he still remembers what it was like, and that makes him different.

He leads me through the busy room until we reach a staircase that winds up to an extremely high second story. The balcony overlooking the downstairs area is far less crowded, and by the time he takes me to a hallway near the back, we're already alone except for the thump of music and fading sound of laughter.

Every step we take into the hallway makes the party grow quieter and quieter, until the near-silence is almost eerie.

"I thought you were going to give me a tour," I say when we stop outside a large set of doors at the end of the hallway. "This looks like a bedroom." Even though I might sound cross with him, the truth is my heart is pounding out of control. I've thought about that night he took me in the club so many times now, about how sweet it felt to surrender to him. Only now, I can't help thinking back to what he said about not wanting kids.

If I knew I could never have kids, would I still be happy?

I don't have time to think about it, because Jayce answers my question about the tour by inserting a key into one of the doors and then swinging it open. My eyebrows climb my forehead as I take in what looks like a private BDSM club in his house.

There's a sleek, modern lounge area decorated in a way that feels warm and sensual--from the deep red fabrics to the polished wood of the full bar. The room is circular with doors in every direction.

"I thought some day I might desire a private place to enjoy my submissive, if I ever found her."

I look at him from the corner of my eyes. "Have you?" I ask.

"I have," he says. "But she's taking her sweet time realizing it."

I look down. "I feel something, Jayce. I really do. I just have so many doubts still. Like all this fear is clogging my head until I can't think straight."

"Then don't think," he says. "Come here. I want to show you a place where you can let your mind rest--well, sort of," he adds with a mischievous grin that makes me nervous.

He takes me through the small lobby to the nearest door and pulls it open. My breath catches when we step into a completely different atmosphere. Soft silk cloth dangles from the ceiling, lit by warm yellow light. We pass through a short hallway as the silk brushes against our skin, trailing behind us. The hallway leads into a bedroom where a four-poster bed dominates the space. Lit candles sit on every surface, adding a warmth to the room and a comforting, pulsing glow of light.

"Wow," I say. "So... you just always have candles burning in here, or were you planning this?" I ask.

I can't tell if it's the lighting, or if Jayce actually blushes at that, but once he closes the door and turns around, I can see the change has already started to come over him. The subtle sense of humor he has come to show me in our time outside the club has somehow left his features until all that's left is the dom I met that first night in his club.

"You said I could choose our date tonight, princess," he says, walking toward me with no particular rush, but the look in his eyes makes his intentions painfully clear.

Doubts bubble up in my mind. I want what he's offering, but I want a family, too. And as much as I know it would just be one more night together, I'm still afraid everything so far has just been me falling into the same old traps I always do where are concerned.

Jayce doesn't give me time to deliberate or think. He surprises me by actually shoving me backwards onto the bed, where it feels like I sink into a cloud. Once I've landed, he sets to stripping out of his jacket, tie, and shirt. I watch with fascination, unable to tear my eyes away from the sight of his buttons being undone and the way his tanned skin glows in the candlelight.

"You've been naughty, princess. I've been keeping track of every time you displeased me, and tonight, you pay the price."

His words make me feel surprisingly ashamed. *I've displeased him?* Oddly enough, the fact that I'm about to be *punished* for displeasing him seems less upsetting to me than the possibility that I haven't been making him happy.

"You feel guilty," he observes, tilting my chin up and studying my face. "Don't. You may think being my submissive is only about sex." As if to contradict his own words, he reaches down--almost unthinkingly--and starts tenderly removing my clothes. "It's not. The sex may be the best you've ever had, but it's not the *point.*"

"What is?" I ask.

"*Sir*," he growls, the sudden change in his face making me suck in surprised breath.

"Sir," I add.

"The point," he continues as if there had been no interruption. "Is that what we will create together goes beyond any traditional relationship can hope to. Together, we'll explore the edge of our limits. We'll push the boundaries until we've discovered *exactly* who we are and what it means for us to be together. There will be no secrets. No lies. When I'm your Dom and you're my submissive, we will be more closely bound than you can imagine."

My skin tingles, and it's not just from the way his fingers brush against it as he pulls my panties down and unclasps my bra until I'm completely naked for him.

"No shame," he says. "No doubts. No regrets. Just two bodies and two minds joining together in the most pure expression of love possible. *Trust*."

I swallow hard. I'm distracted from the perfect future he promises by two glaring problems. I still don't know if I'm pregnant, and even if I'm not, he won't want to give me kids. Everything he says sounds amazing, yet I don't know if it would be enough to give up my dream of a family.

Guilt swirls in my stomach as I nod anyway, too drunk on the moment to spoil everything right now. I convince myself I'll find some way to come to terms with it when I've had time to think, that it's just the effect he has on me making it so hard to puzzle out how this could work or lead to a happy future for me.

"Get on your knees for me, princess."

His words bounce around in my head without meaning for a few seconds. I'm too distracted by my wandering thoughts and my fears to react.

"I won't ask twice," he says suddenly.

The sound of his voice snaps through the fog in my brain. My body moves to obey him now without question. I turn over, climbing to my hands and knees, presenting my ass to him like a prize waiting to be claimed.

A strange, creeping sense of calm comes over me. I can't explain it, but when I'm surrendering to him, it feels like life loosens its grip on me so I can breathe again and my problems seem distant.

"Let go," he says, running a finger down my spine as he stands beside me on the bed. "Your inhibitions are only getting in the way. Trust your submission to me again for tonight, princess. Be mine. My submissive, *my property*. Let me use you..."

I close my eyes. All I can manage is a soft sound between a moan and a quick breath, but it seems to be enough for him.

"But first, it's time for your punishment."

He reaches under the bed and comes up with a leather paddle. I can't keep my eyes from it as he brings it up and gradually drags it down my back and ass before brushing the already wet lips of my pussy with its edge. I shiver. Goosebumps rise up across my body in the wake of its touch, and my ass is already tingling with the expectation of contact

"You've made me wait too long for this, princess..."

He brings the paddle down on my bare ass, making me lurch forward and gasp. It stings almost like a swarm of bees got me for a few moments, he doesn't wait for the pain to fully subside before he brings it down again on the other side of my ass this time. "You knew I wouldn't approve of your friend coming on our date, but you brought her anyway."

I sink down to my forearms, eyes squeezed shut against the sting of the paddle.

"But," he says, leaning closer to my ass until his breath brushes the tender skin where he paddled me. He plants a soothing kiss on the spot, melting the pain down until it blends together into something strange and wonderful. "I enjoyed the date very much. More than I thought I would." He kisses the other side, until I'm left with only a swirling excitement that gathers between my legs, making my need for his even more intimate attention that much greater.

"You've also been very disrespectful," he says, standing back up and moving to gather one of the candles by the bed. He brings it closer to me, holding it near his face so the flickering light casts his features in an orange glow. "And you must be punished until you learn to show me the proper respect. To address me as Sir. To heed my commands without question."

"Turn over and lie on your back," he says, setting the candle on the nightstand. I do as he says quickly, not wanting to disappoint him again.

He nods. It's a small gesture, but when he makes the subtle shift from Jayce to my dom, I'm dragged into a world where the only thing that matters is pleasing him. The only pleasure or satisfaction comes from making my dom happy, in surrendering completely and trusting his guidance to be the truth. So even his slight nod is enough to send a surge of excitement and pleasure through me as I position myself on my back, lying flat while he takes his time appreciating the sight of my body.

"Gorgeous," he says. He runs a finger down from my breast to my pussy, lifting his touch just before he reaches my clit in a way that can't be accidental. I can sense that he wants to drag this out, and I can't say I'm upset by the realization. "I couldn't have made you any more perfect myself. Every line," he says, palming my breast and squeezing firmly. "Every curve." He grips the inside of my thigh, urging my legs open for him. "Even the way you smell," he says, bending to kiss my mound as he breathes in deeply. "*Sublime.*"

I take in a shuddering breath, my back arching involuntarily as if my body is offering itself up to him.

"You were made for me, princess," he says. He pulls a pair of handcuffs from under the bed and dangles them for me to see.

"Cell by cell and inch by inch, you were built to be mine." He pulls my arms over my head and clamps one cuff around my wrist, threads the other through the headboard, and then clamps my other wrist. Thankfully, the cuffs have a black fuzzy material around the metal, so even when he secures them tightly, they aren't uncomfortable.

"Now that I'm sure you're not going anywhere..." He picks up the candle again, lifting it above my stomach and lets a drop of wax fall just above my navel.

I flinch from the sudden heat, but much like drips of cold water, the intensity is momentary before it gives way to only the subtle reminder of heat. A tight circle forms as the wax cools and solidifies on my skin .

"And I was made to claim you," he says, finishing his earlier thought and meeting my eyes with so much intensity I can't seem to look away, even as I can sense the next drop of wax pooling at the end of the candle.

It patters down just below my breasts, shocking me again with a temporary burst of heat followed by a warm tightness. The next drop falls on my nipple, and the heat is so intense on the sensitive skin there that I gasp. It's unpleasant for a second, maybe two, then an unfamiliar sensation spreads through me. Maybe this is what he was talking about--the intimacy of exploring the edge of my desires with him and trusting him to be my guide. It's almost as if I've split away part of my mind in this moment. The part that normally steps in when things go outside my comfort zone and puts it to a stop. Right now I can almost feel Jayce's presence within me, like he's taking the control and the responsibility of that job from me.

Instead of the fear I would normally expect the realization to bring, it only makes my pussy throb with need and my chest fill with the most wonderful warmth. *I'm his right now. Completely and totally his. I only have to please him.*

I lose track of time as drop by drop of scorching wax covers my skin. I grow used to the sensation of heat and the gradual fade to warmth and the tight sensation of a growing coating of wax covers my body. When he starts to let drops of wax fall on my mound and my inner thighs, the heat feels so much more intense, but I don't stop him. I let the heat come and I embrace the warmth. The last drop lands so dangerously close to my clit that I finally get ready to say something, maybe even one of the safe words. It's as if he really does have some way of knowing my thoughts because sets the candle down on the bedside and looks back to my body, which is covered in drops of wax from my breasts to my pussy.

"Now the best part," he says. "It's time to clean you up."

I bite my lip, watching as he slips out of his pants and briefs before climbing on top of me. I raise my eyebrows when he bends to use his mouth to gently work the wax away with his lips and tongue. "Is that safe to put in your mouth?" I ask.

He looks up at me with a sly expression before chewing and swallowing. "Safe and delicious. It's edible, princess."

"Oh." I lean back, grinning in excited anticipation of the process ahead of him. Every drop of wax that dropped down on me is now a point of contact where his lips and tongue scour my body bit by bit. I feel him move off me to grab something else from under the bed. When I bend my neck to look up, I see him holding two jars. One is full of chocolate syrup and the other is full of whipped cream.

I laugh in surprise. "What else is under the bed?"

He smirks, dipping a spoon in the syrup and raising it so it drizzles back into the jar. "I made sure the room was equipped with everything I'd need before we arrived. And what can I say, I have a sweet tooth. What about you?" he asks, lifting the spoon again.

"Please, sir," I say hungrily.

I expect him to bring the spoon to my mouth, but instead he straddles me so that his erect cock is only inches from my lips.

"I was thinking something sweeter, but I won't complain," I say.

He picks up the jar of syrup and drizzles it over the head of his cock until the excess drips down my chest, running in warm path between my breasts.

"I hope you came hungry tonight, princess."

10

JAYCE

I let my eyes close as she wraps her hot mouth around my cock, licking up the syrup like a good little submissive. She doesn't show any sign of wanting to stop, even when the syrup is all gone. I let her continue to suck me off, occasionally adding more syrup to my cock when I think she's done a good enough job to deserve the sweet reward, but my own appetite eventually gets the better of me.

I want to see Miley moaning and begging me for more. I want her so fucking horny that her juices are leaking from that tight little pussy and she can't keep her moans quiet.

I dip the spoon in the syrup and pull away, loving the pouty look she gives when I take my cock from her. I drizzle syrup across her tits and her stomach, all the way down to the creases where her legs meet her pussy. Once I'm done, I add a dollop of whipped cream to her nipples and mound for no other reason than the fact that I love the taste. And I know the cold contrast will add another layer to her experience.

She writhes in the most sexy fucking way imaginable, constantly biting her full bottom lip and letting it pop back out all pink and flushed. I dip my thumb in the chocolate and smear it across her lips before sucking them into my mouth and licking her clean. I kiss my way from her jaw down to her neck and her tits, licking and kissing up every last drop of syrup and cream, taking my time as I do, knowing she's loving every last second of it.

By the time I reach her lower stomach, she's gasping and squirming against me, hips rising off the bed in her desperation to have my attention on her pussy. My cock throbs just thinking how wet she must already be for me and how good it would feel to bury myself inside her again. Not yet, though. Soon, but not yet.

I run my tongue down her mound, paying special attention to the syrup that found its way into the crease between her pussy and inner thigh, letting my tongue move so close to her folds that she must be ready to lose her mind.

"Please, sir," she gasps. "I need it."

I look up from between her legs, enjoying the view of her body still glistening from the work I've done cleaning her up and her hands cuffed to the headboard above her head. "Tell me what you need, princess. Beg me for it."

"I need your mouth. Your cock. Your fingers. Whatever you'll give me. But I need to cum so bad it hurts."

"Since you forgot to call me Sir," I say tauntingly. "It's going to keep hurting a little longer."

I scoop out some whipped cream and smear it on her toes, which I take into my mouth and suck clean one by one. She closes her eyes and presses her head back into the pillows, lips parting beautifully for me. I let my eyes wander to her slick pussy, which looks so undeniably ready for my cock that I know I've reached the limits of my patience. I need to have her, to take her, to own every fucking inch of her tight little hole.

I grab a condom from beside the bed and slip it on, noticing an odd expression on Miley's face as I do. Maybe she was hoping I'd take her unprotected again, but I can't take the chance. That was a mistake. A reckless mistake. I can't afford to get Miley pregnant and risk her health because of my selfish desire to have a child. Maybe that's over-the-top, but the guilt I feel over my mother's death sticks with me every day of my life. Along with it comes the fear that I could do the same thing to the woman I love.

No fucking way. No kids. No pregnancy. No risk to my princess. I don't care how good her having my baby might sound. It's just not a risk I can take. So she can give me that pouty look all she wants, but I'm wearing a rubber.

Her disappointment is forgotten when I grip the base of my cock and give it to her in one powerful thrust. She takes in a quick burst of air through her nose and her eyes shoot open. I know she'll feel a slight pain from being entered so suddenly, a stretching sensation maybe, but it will pass. When it does, the pleasure will seem that much more intense by contrast.

"You like that, princess?" I ask.

"Mhmm," she moans.

I bend my neck to suck her nipple into my mouth, biting slightly before I pull away. It should sting for a moment--long enough to remind her to fucking call me Sir.

"Sir," she says like a good girl.

I grin, pulling her legs up higher so I can get even deeper inside her. She digs her heels into my ass, pulling me in with each thrust, begging me for every inch of cock I'll give her and more.

"Jayce," she gasps.

I want to draw this out, to make her wait for more, to make her beg until her throat is hoarse, but I can't stop myself. I drive myself into her again and again, drawing out the most delicious moans from her with every thrust of my hips. When I feel her walls tighten around me and her body tenses, my own orgasm comes roaring from me. I keep fucking her until I've emptied every last drop of my cum inside the condom and she's lying breathless and still.

Once I've thrown away the condom and slipped my pants back on, I move back to Miley, who is waiting so beautifully for me on the bed with her hands still cuffed. I unlock them and check her wrists for any sign of bruising or chafing. There's a slight indent from where the cuffs pressed into the base of her palms, so I apply lotion and rub the area until I see some of the color return to her skin.

"I like how you look after me when we've finished, sir," she says.

I favor her with a smile to let her know she did well remembering to pay me the proper respect. *For once.* But I actually enjoy that she's still prone to moments of defiance. My idea of the perfect submissive has always been one who wants to please me above all else, but who also has a mischievous side and tempts my wrath from time to time. As with everything else, Miley fits the mold of what I want perfectly in that regard.

"Of course," I say, moving my attention now to all the places I dripped wax across her body. Her skin is slightly pink in some areas. It would pass in a few minutes without my help, but I take the excuse to apply more lotion to my hands and rub it into her soft skin, spending more time than I need to on her breasts. "What we do together is about control, above all else. I don't expect that I will ever do anything to cause you true harm, but it's important for me to make sure there were no accidents. No rashes, no bruises, no cuts. I have to be sure you're as perfect as you were the moment you submitted to me."

"Well, I like it," she says, smiling up at me. "It feels nice. I never really had this kind of gentleness in my life. My dad was always hard on us. *So hard,*" she says, looking distantly toward a group of candles by the wall. "Nothing ever made him happy. He demanded so much and I think for a long time I tried to make him happy. I wanted to be his good little girl because I was silly enough to think *that* was the problem. He wasn't abusive because he was just an asshole to me back then, it was because I wasn't ever good enough. But when I would do exactly what he wanted, he always seemed to change the rules at the last minute. That was the thing. I could never win. I could never make him happy. Eventually, I figured out the truth, but it was only after so many wasted years."

"I'm sorry," I say, cupping her cheek and kissing her forehead. "You know you've pleased me very much tonight though, don't you?"

"Yes, Sir," she says, smiling shyly at me. Her expression fades into dejection as she looks down. "I must sound so creepy right now. Like I'm using you as some kind of substitute for my dad that I could never please, but--"

"No," I say. "It's not creepy or strange. It's normal. Everybody has unresolved issues from their past, and if they say they don't, they're either lying or oblivious. Hell, I think that's most of the point in being an adult. You're trying to find a way to move beyond the demons in your past, whatever way that is. Some people ignore them, some embrace them, and some overcome them. This is an outlet for you, Miley. It's cathartic because it helps you heal. Never be ashamed of that. Do you understand me? That's a command," I add with a little mock seriousness.

She flashes me a crooked smile, nodding her head but wiping at her eyes.

"I mean it," I say, cupping her face and lifting her chin so she's looking at me. I wipe a tear from the corner of her eye and kiss her tenderly, longingly. "This is what you need it to be. There's never any reason to be ashamed of that."

"What is it for you?" she asks.

I chuckle, letting my hands fall and taking my turn studying the ground. She's perceptive, I'll give her that, but right now I wish she wasn't. I can't exactly tell her to embrace her past and how good a thing it is while also hiding my own from her. So I suck up my reluctance and start talking.

"For me? I think there are two parts to it. On one hand, it lets the little, skinny kid from my past take control. There were times when I looked at my life and how everything was happening around me and I'd just think how I had no power over any of it. Things could go to complete shit, and it wouldn't matter how hard I wanted or tried, it'd happen anyway. So maybe part of it is right there. This world is a place where I can take that control back. And if I can take control here, it helps me feel like there's a little more sense to the rest of it, I guess."

She nods. "That makes sense. And what is the other part?"

"The other part is that I thought one day I'd find a submissive who needed something very specific from her dom. Not just sex. Not just cold domination. Not even just passion. I wanted a submissive who was nearly broken and at the edge of her ability to resist. Someone beautifully flawed--just barely holding on when it seemed like everything was out of her control and the world didn't care how much she wanted or tried. I wanted to find that woman and show her there is control. There is order. There is a place where she can let go and trust in someone else to be her guide. I wanted to find you," I say.

More tears well in her eyes and she leans her head down onto my shoulder, wrapping her small arms around my back.

"You're the one I've been looking for all this time," I whisper. "My perfect submissive. My perfect woman. The woman I love," I say.

My own words send a cold shock through me. I hadn't planned to say so much, to reveal everything like I just did. But now that the words have come out of me, I feel the expectation hanging between us like electricity. Will she say it too? Can she?

She's crying harder now. *Fuck*, I think. My stomach is sinking and feels cold. She doesn't feel the same way. As much as I've read into her thoughts and behavior, I've been wrong. I was so sure everything between us was mutual, and now I've laid it out on the table and she's flinching, unwilling to commit to what I've offered her.

"I'm so sorry," she says suddenly, pulling away and getting off the bed to find her clothes, which she hastily slips back into. "I can't be what you need me to be. I want it. I really do. But it wouldn't last forever. It couldn't."

I'm too stunned to speak. I can only watch as she moves to the door and takes one last, longing look back at me. In that moment I can see she's about to say something, and I lean forward, waiting for the words because my own won't seem to come.

Her expression changes and she looks back toward the door, stepping halfway out to the hallway. "I'm sorry," she says again before closing the door.

The door closing snaps me out of my surprise. I jump up from the bed and chase after her, not even taking the time to put my shirt back on. I see just a glimpse of her heel disappearing out of view at the end of the hallway and run to catch up with her.

She's moving down the stairs as fast as she can, making me nervous as hell that she's going to trip and fall down in her hurry to get away from me.

Fuck. The thought makes my stomach turn. Somehow, some way I turned into the thing I wanted to protect her from, the kind of thing that made her want to run.

I catch up with her at the bottom of the stairs, drawing a fair amount of attention from my lack of a shirt, but it's not the craziest thing people have seen at one of my parties, so their attention is only momentary.

"Miley," I say once I'm just behind her and able to grab her arm.

She tries to pull away from me and I instinctively grip harder, not wanting her to get away before I can find out what's wrong.

"Let go!" she cries, pulling again.

"Miley, just let me--" I say, reaching for her other arm.

She brings her hand up and slaps me hard enough that the sound rises above the music, making anyone who wasn't already watching the spectacle stop what they're doing to look now.

My hand falls away from her arm and she hurries outside, pulling out her phone--probably to call someone to come pick her up.

"At least let me give you a ride home," I say, even as my cheek stings from the slap.

She gives me a look over her shoulder that I can't entirely make sense of. I see sorrow and regret in her features, maybe fear. She closes the front door behind her, leaving me to feel that special kind of alone you can only feel in such a crowded place.

"You okay?" Leo asks squattingdown beside me at the bottom of the stairs.

I didn't even realize I had sunk down to sit with my back against the bannister. I look over at him, ignoring the curious faces turned our way.

"Should I be?" I ask.

He chuckles, then sits down cross-legged in front of me, which is an odd sight to see from such a big man. It has been a long fucking time since Leo had to look out for me, but I can see him slipping back into the role effortlessly. He's my big brother, and in so many ways he was always a shield for me. I thought I'd outgrown the need for that side of him, but Miley walking away makes it feel like someone just ripped a handful of my heart away.

"Depends," he says. "Did you fuck up?"

"That's what I'm asking myself," I say distantly.

"Ah," he says knowingly. "A mystery mistake?"

I nod.

"Damn," he says. "Those are fucking tough. But hey, it can only be so many things, right?"

"Uh," I say doubtfully. "She's a woman, Leo. I'm pretty sure it can basically be *any* of the things."

He grins. "I mean if you break it down by category of fuck ups. There's really just a few broad categories when it comes to relationships. Think about it. You've got things you did, and things you didn't do that she wanted you to. Oh, and things you said or things you didn't say," he adds, sounding a little less confident that this is as simple as he was making it sound. "And I guess there's things she has come to realize you'll never do--or things she realizes you'll never *stop* doing. I'm not really helping, am I?"

I grin. "Not really."

He makes a sour face, nodding. "Hey," he says more seriously. "Just give her a couple days. I know you probably want to go kick her door down or some other heroically stupid kind of thing right now, but maybe she just needs a few days to appreciate how much happier she was when she was with you."

"A couple days? Fuck, man. I was going to go over once she had time to get a ride home."

Leo raises his eyebrows at me like a scornful parent. "So she runs away from you at the party, won't even ride home with you, and you think she's going to be happy to see you knocking at her door in an hour?"

"Dammit," I growl, spearing a hand through my hair. "Then I'll wait till tomorrow."

"Jayce. I'm saying this because you're my brother and I'm trying to look out for you. You've got to let her breathe for a couple days. Give it some time. You know what they say, absence makes the heart grow fonder."

"Yeah? Does your heart feel pretty fond for dad?" I ask.

Leo glares at me. "Did I say abandon her and never come back?"

I sigh. "So you're suggesting I just *wait*?"

"At least a few days. Give her some time to cool off."

"I'll give her until tomorrow afternoon," I say stonily.

Leo laughs. "Yeah. That's probably about how long I'd be able to wait, too." He claps me on the shoulder and stands. "You lovebirds will figure it out. Don't worry."

11

MILEY

I watch out the window as hills roll by. Kyle and I have driven this route enough for me to know in about an hour, the hills will give way to the forested mountains that have been the site of countless camping trips.

We used to come out here to the wilderness all the time up until a few years ago. I guess our lives got too busy or we drifted apart, but one way or another we stopped coming. Until I came home from Jayce's party last night and asked Kyle to call out of work for a week so we could get away. It was definitely impulsive of me and immature on more levels than one, but I can't face him.

I know in my heart that I want a family. I want to have little kids running around my ankles. I want to cuddle babies, cry when I watch my kids get on the bus for their first day of school, and I want to be there crying like a baby when they graduate high school. Jayce felt like the perfect guy in every single way, except that he doesn't want to give me the family I need. It's a non-negotiable. I know that, but I also know if given a chance, he'd end up making me want to try things with him anyway.

It might be fine for a few months or maybe even a few years, but eventually I'd know I had given the keys of my heart to a man who didn't want to go to the same place I do.

"So," Kyle says from the driver's seat of the truck. "Are you planning on telling me the real reason we're doing this on such short notice? Or am I supposed to keep believing you just really missed camping all of the sudden?"

I sigh. There was a time not too long ago that I wouldn't have ever hid anything from Kyle, back when we were still living with dad. I can't put my finger on what changed exactly, but at some point it felt like he had to turn into our dad to help us escape, almost like the brother I knew permanently sacrificed part of himself for me. Now when I look at him, I see moments and glimpses of our dad behind his eyes, and it wakes up all the old instincts to stay quiet and not open up.

I owe him more than sulky silence though, so I decide to suck it up and start talking. "I needed to get away for a few days so Jayce couldn't talk me into getting back together with him," I say.

Kyle half-turns, raising an eyebrow. "Didn't realize you two broke up."

It irks me that I hear a slight hint of relief or excitement in his tone, but I shouldn't be surprised. In all honesty, I think Kyle would like it best if I went the rest of my life single. Maybe I shouldn't blame him though, considering my track record. I've probably been an overprotective brother's worst nightmare, but it was never intentional. It feels dumb to think it now, but when I look back on all my relationship troubles, it always started with me thinking this guy would be the one who was really good to me--the one who was different. Surprise, surprise. That's exactly how I felt when I met Jayce. But he *was* good to me. Just not good *for* me.

"I'm not sure if Jayce realizes either," I say.

Kyle chuckles. "What, you're just ghosting him?"

"He's obnoxiously persuasive," I say, but my justification sounds thin, even to my own ears. "If I tried to tell him flat-out, he'd just talk me out of it. That's mostly why I want to get away. With a week to clear my head and get him off my mind, I will be able to stand my ground when we come back. I'll tell him it's not going to work and we'll both be able to move on."

"I could tell him for you, you know."

"I know I'm not exactly handling this like a mature adult right now, but I'm not ready to revert all the way back to middle school level. I just need time to make sure my head is clear before I talk to him again."

"Well, here I was thinking you wanted to spend time with your big brother."

"I do. I could've just come up here by myself, couldn't I?"

"Yeah, except you've never be able to put up your tent or start a fire without my help. I feel so used," he says with a grin.

I glare at him. "I'm pretty sure I can figure out how to put up my own tent."

"Yeah? I guess we'll find out."

Two Weeks Later

I wait for what seems like ages while the pregnancy test indicator gradually fades into view. I didn't feel ready to come back after a week like I had originally planned, so it turned into two. I let my phone die so I wouldn't be tempted to take any of Jayce's calls or texts, which started pouring in the day after we left. I only just plugged it in an hour ago when Kyle and I got back, exhausted and thankful for air conditioners and solid walls after so many days outside.

My period should have come a week into our camping trip, but all the pads and tampons I brought along are still unopened in my camping bag.

This is the first pregnancy test I've ever used, and I stupidly imagined it would be a special moment. I never thought I'd be hunched over on the toilet, hands shaking because I'm so scared of what it will mean if that faint blue color forms into a plus sign. Even if it's a negative, I'm not usually late on my period, so I'll be worried it was just a false negative since I'm taking the test on the early side.

My stomach sinks when what was starting to look like a minus sign sprouts a little bit of blue that begins to stretch upwards and downwards. *Positive.*

I drop the test on the ground, but the positive sign keeps growing darker and more clear, as if it needed to make the message any easier to see.

I'm pregnant.

I cup my face in my hands, breathing out long, shuddering breath after long, shuddering breath. I have to tell him. I don't know how in hell I'm going to do it, but he needs to know it's his. Whether he wants to be part of this babies life or not, he needs to know, and that terrifies me to my core.

All my life I've been searching for a man who will accept me and treat me well, and I think in a large part it's because my dad never accepted me. So I've felt desperate to find a man who would. Now the only man who ever seemed to accept me is going to learn that something he doesn't want is growing inside me.

The worst part is I know I won't be able to tell him right away. I just ran off from him for two weeks without so much as a text to let him know where I was going, and he has no idea that in my mind we had broken up. I run my fingers through my hair and hang my head. Leave it to me to take the perfect guy and make this big of a mess, to be this stupid and impulsive.

Somehow I'm going to have to find the courage to tell him the truth. I just hope I can do it before things go too far again, before I let him suck me back into his dark, beautiful world.

12

JAYCE

I knock on the door to Miley's apartment. I checked with her landlord last week and she didn't move out, so I've just been hoping like hell she'll come back, because she hasn't returned my calls or my texts. I've lost track of how many times I've yelled at Leo for suggesting I give her time. If I had just come to her fucking apartment that night like I was planning, I bet I could've caught her before she left.

Now I've spent the last two weeks like some kind of stalker. I've been coming by her apartment every day, sometimes more than once, knocking and waiting for her to open the door so I can have a chance to figure out why she's blowing me off.

If I was a better man, I'd say I wasn't pissed. The truth is I'm angry with her. Regardless of what she's been through or dealing with, she should've known she could trust me enough to talk with me about it. Blowing me off like this was bullshit, and I'm not going to promise myself I'll go easy on her for it.

The door swings open and all my anger disappears the moment I see her face. Her hair's a mess and she looks flustered, but I've wanted to see her so badly now for what feels like so long, she looks more beautiful than she ever has. I step forward, wrapping her in a tight hug. "You're okay," I say. "I was worried about you."

She stands stiffly, letting me hug her for a few seconds before her arms slide around my back and then tighten. When I pull back I can see the conflict in her face--the pain. All the anger I felt about her leaving without notice feels impossible to call back up. Whatever she's dealing with, it's real, and it's powerful. "Help me understand," I say. "I can't help if I don't know."

The change in her face is so sudden I can almost believe it's real. She smiles, blowing out a quick breath and straightening her hair with her hands. "Sorry," she says. "I was just taking a nap. I must look terrifying."

"Never," I say.

She smiles with a touch of sadness, then chews her lip. "Look. I owe you an explanation. A big one. Running off like that without talking to you about it wasn't right. It wasn't even close to right. I needed to clear my head a little bit, and I could've at least told you that much."

"You could've," I agree. "But if you're not ready to talk about it, I can wait. *For a little while*," I add.

She smiles with relief. "I will talk to you about it. I promise. I just need a little more time."

"Yes, you will," I say. I want to be gentle for her. To give her the time she needs... but she made me wait too fucking long. Two weeks without my princess. Two weeks without so much as a taste of her. There will be time for healing, soft words, and talk. Later, though. "And you've disappointed me. You will be at my house tonight by seven. You'll be wearing a white dress with white cotton panties and no bra. I'll text you the code to let yourself in, and when I come home, I expect to find you waiting for me. You remember the room I took you in during the party? You'll use the door beside that and wait for me on your hands and knees. You'll wait as long as it takes for me to come, because you need to understand what it was like not knowing. Am I clear?"

Her eyes are wide and her lips are parted. All the dirty parts of her mind are screaming in delight at how completely I'm planning to take control of her. I can practically see it in her face. She licks her lips though, hesitating.

"Don't make me ask twice," I warn.

She nods quickly. "Y-yes. But I don't have any white dresses."

"The clothing and jewelry I expect you to wear will be delivered within the next few hours," I say.

As much as I want to stay longer and enjoy her presence, now that I know she's back I can think only of the discipline she needs. She needs to be brought back in line, and she needs to be reminded how good it feels to give me the reins, even if it's just for a night.

"Yes, sir," she says softly.

I grin as I turn and leave, closing the door behind me. I can't say how I know, but I can tell she wasn't expecting our interaction to go that way. All for the better, though. She needs to learn that she's my submissive, and nothing will ever feel so right to her as obedience. She'll also learn the more she fights my control, the tighter her leash will become, and the more she obeys, the more freedom she will have.

WHEN I FINALLY ARRIVE HOME THAT NIGHT, IT'S FIFTEEN MINUTES after seven. I could barely think straight all day from knowing that Miley would be putting on the outfit I sent her, slipping into the pair of panties I commanded her to wear. The thought of her arriving at my place and walking through the empty house to wait for me how I told her to and exactly where I told her to... *fuck*, just imagining it has my cock so hard it hurts.

I received a notification when she arrived at my house and let herself in with the keypad. Exactly one minute early like a good girl.

Beneath the excitement, I feel a creeping kind of guilt. When I first saw Miley, I knew she was damaged. I told myself the only thing I'd ever care about if I had her was to help her become whole again, to heal her and give her the kind of relationship she deserves. When I saw her earlier today, it was like the cracks I had begun to see smooth over in her life had reopened, and even though part of me thought the best way to help her heal might be to sit down, have a normal night, and let her talk... I convinced myself it would be better for her to submit to me.

It wasn't an entirely selfish idea, but I can't lie to myself and say my own lust after having her away for two weeks didn't play into the decision. I do think the answers she needs to find inside herself may only come while she's under my complete control and has surrendered to me. If she's able to completely let go of her inhibitions, she will be forced to face the truths she has been hiding from, whatever they are. I know that much is true, and yet I still can't shake the guilt that having her come here for me wasn't entirely selfless.

My guilty conscience fades into background noise when I open the double doors to my private rooms, where each door leads to a different theme.

I walk through the area I think of as the lobby, passing the bar and the private table until I reach the door to the dark room. Of course, it's not dark when I open the door, because I wanted to make sure I had a chance to appreciate my princess presenting herself to me, and *fuck* am I glad I left the lights on.

The dress I bought for her is a lacey white thing that flares out at the hem just slightly, and like I had hoped, when she's bent over for me, it rides up enough that I can see a hint of her pussy covered by the white cotton panties I wanted her to wear. She stirs when the door opens, but like a good little submissive, she doesn't turn around or say a word.

She waits while I walk toward her, not even moving when I kneel to get the most spectacular view of the wet spot already staining her panties. The doubts I had about my choice to have her come here for me melt away. She wants this. She wants it so badly that kneeling here for me for fifteen minutes has her wet enough to soak her panties.

"Tell me, princess," I say, walking toward the door and turning off the lights.

She gasps in surprise, because the room was designed to be completely and totally black without the lights on. She wouldn't even see her hands in front of her face right now.

"Tell me what you were imagining I would do to you that has you so wet," I say.

"I knew you were going to be upset with me, and that you would punish me," she says.

My cock stirs at her admission. "And that's all?" I ask. "You knew I would punish you, and that brought you pleasure?"

"Yes."

"Why?"

"Because I know I deserve it." She pauses, and I hear her throat click as she swallows, hesitating. "It makes me feel good to know that I can make you happy. Like this," she says, and I can't see it, but I can practically picture her hanging her head, as if what she's doing is something to be ashamed of. "It feels good to know you're going to take control, because when I have control, all I can do is mess things up. *Sir*," she adds.

"Listen to me very carefully," I say. "I don't take control of your life. I take a part of you that you bring to this room, and I demand submission for that moment in time. When you're here with me and you call me Sir, I demand everything. After a while, you will begin to leave our experiences together feeling more trust in yourself than you ever felt before. It won't be me that is guiding your life and making your decisions. It will be you.

"You'll learn that you are the master of your own mind

because you did what so few can truly do. You surrendered. You didn't give up or quit. You *surrendered*. You had the power and the control in your hands and you willingly gave it to me, even if it was only a few hours, you felt what it was like to be without power. Once you've felt that, you'll never look at your own power the same again, you'll understand how much control you truly have and how much you can do with it. That's the gift our time together will give to you, princess."

"There's something I need to tell you, sir," she says quietly.

"Not now," I growl. "You're mine, princess. You came into my house. You walked into my private rooms. You're wearing the clothes, jewelry, and underwear just like I ordered you to. You're even kneeling down for me like I asked. You've never belonged to anyone like you belong to me right now, and you never will belong to anyone else. So long as these lights are off, I own you, body and soul, so whatever it is you think I need to know can wait, because I have been waiting too long to hear you begging for my cock."

There's a small sound, almost as if she starts to speak but thinks better of it. "Good," I say when it's clear she has given up trying to speak. I see nothing at all, only pure darkness so thick it feels as though it's actually inside my head, and it's fucking thrilling.

"You'll notice your other senses begin to compensate when one is taken away. Sounds become more clear. More crisp," I say, tugging the knot loose on my tie and letting it slip to the floor. I add my shirt to the growing pile, followed shortly by the rest of my clothes until I'm completely naked.

I take practiced steps to the far wall, six strides and I'm within reach of the large feather on my right. I can't see it, but I know it's an incredibly soft, black feather on the end of a leather handle. I pluck it from the wall, then retrace my steps to stand exactly where I was before.

I breathe in deeply, already feeling as though my nose is more responsive than usual, because I can even smell the scent of her soft skin beneath her perfume. "You'll notice even the slightest touch," I say, extending my arm out until I feel the warmth of her skin beneath the back of her dress. I splay my hand, letting it slide up her bare back, where I slip the shoulder straps off. "Feels magnified." I gently work her free of the dress, not rushing because I'm savoring the anticipation. Every second I draw this out will only make the reward that much greater for both of us.

"You'll feel as though time slows down, because your body is used to writing memories down with your eyes. We *see* our memories. Right now, your brain is being forced to create a new kind of experience, and that change makes it feel slower to you, more drawn out. Every second drags in the most exquisite way." I pull her dress down to her hips, dragging just the tip of a feather along her spine as I do in a way I know will make her feel chills across her entire body.

"Your skin will respond to every single touch by sending blood rushing to the spot, activating nerves and synapses in your brain until even the slightest point of contact will be crystal clear to you." I yank the dress down to her knees, working each leg free until I've tossed it aside and have her in nothing but her panties and heels.

I can't see a damn thing, but the memory of her bending over for me is so clear I can still picture how breathtaking she looks right now. I do the next best thing, and use my free hand to explore her nearly naked body. I pay special attention to her soaked panties. The way her juices slick the cotton material makes my dick feel like it's so hard it could fucking explode.

But I can only wait so long before I strip her panties too, tossing them into the darkness along with her shoes.

I grip her ass with my hand, letting my thumb graze her slick folds. She feels so unbelievably good that it's all I can do not to slide my fingers inside her now and lick up her sweet juices. Not yet. "Time is a tool as effective as pain if used correctly," I say, drawing the edge of the feather from the top of her ass down to her clit. I want to prime her body for my touch until she'll nearly be ready to cum the first time I put my fingers inside her.

"The longer you have to wait for what you want, the more responsive your body will be. The more desperate you'll be for my cock stuffing that tight pussy."

She lets out the sexiest breath that's halfway between a moan and a sigh. I grin into the darkness, still torturing her with the faintest touch of the feather.

"Now it's time for your real punishment," I say. Without giving her time to brace herself or mentally prepare, I slap her firmly on the ass.

She gasps, probably jolting forward from the shock of the sudden impact. I slap her again on the other cheek, not stopping until I've spanked her three times on each cheek and I know her ass will be stinging. Normally, I only want the pain to last a few seconds, but this time, I wanted my princess to feel the sting so she knows how much she disappointed me when she left these last two weeks. I want her to know there's a price for misbehaving. Though I can only stomach the thought of so much, and I need to be sure she's doing okay with the pain, because she's not saying a word.

"Do you need lotion to soothe it?" I ask.

"No, sir," she says quickly.

I smile with pleasure. She's so willing to accept her punishment and it's turning her on--I can hear it in the strained sound of her voice.

"Good. Now I want you to do something for me."

"Anything, sir."

"Surprise me," I say with a wicked grin.

It's a few seconds before I hear the sound of her movement in the dark, and a few more seconds before I feel her hands fumbling for me. She touches my knees first, then her hands gradually work their way up my thighs, where she grips the base of my cock with one hand and immediately plunges her hot, wet mouth down on my cock.

My head rolls back. *So fucking ready to suck my cock.* I absolutely love it. She works my entire length, not just sucking the head but running her tongue and lips down to the base of my cock and even surprising me when she starts giving special attention to my balls.

"Goddamn," I growl.

I can hear every sound, from the soft, barely audible moans vibrating through my cock to the occasional sucking sound when she pulls her lips away from me. I know she must look so sexy with her lips wrapped around my length that I'm tempted to turn on the lights, but I have enough self-control to suppress the impulse.

It's not long before I'm struggling to keep from filling her mouth with my cum--not that I'm opposed to the idea, of course. I just don't want it to stop yet. I'm not even close to being through with her.

I clench my fists, trying to distract my mind from the sensation of her mouth on me until I can force my impending orgasm back down. I'd stop her, but from the sound of it, she's enjoying herself as much as I am.

I last another minute before I finally grip a handful of her hair at the back of her head and pull her off at the last second. I close my eyes, trying not to imagine how her lips and my cock are probably glistening wet right now, or how I bet her pussy is probably so wet she's dripping for me. I barely manage, but I hold back the orgasm and then breathe out a sigh of relief.

"I think I might forgive you," I say.

She makes a small, but satisfied sound, knowing better than to speak now. She's in my good graces, and she likely knows that means she's finally going to get what she wants.

13

MILEY

My lips are sore from stretching to fit his cock in my mouth and my jaw is cramping, but I barely feel it. When he turned the lights off, it was permission to be someone else for a few hours.To pretend I'm not pregnant and that he isn't likely to toss me aside when he finds out, or that I'm not doing something disgraceful by letting him use me like this one last time, even though I fear he wouldn't if he knew the truth.

I'm on my knees still with no idea where he is, exactly, but he's still gripping my hair so that my head is tilted back. I'm completely as his mercy. By now, I couldn't even find the door in this absolute darkness if I tried, and there's no way I'd be able to free myself from the iron grip he has on my hair.

Instead of frightening me, the lack of control is making my skin buzz with a constant hum of excitement. Combined with the way he made me feel when he dragged that feather across my skin, it really does feel like my sense of touch has transcended what should be possible. I feel everything, down to the the way each tiny hair on my arm reacts to the soft breeze from the air conditioner.

Most of all, my pussy throbs with a kind of need I've never

felt, not even the times I was with Jayce before. Having him in my mouth only made it worse, until I would willingly do anything just to have him inside me, filling me in that perfect way he does, until it seems like I couldn't possibly take any more of him and he couldn't possibly have any more to give, but he does. He'll shift his hips and my legs and another inch will drive into me. I want it so badly.

"Please, sir," I say quietly. To speak louder than a whisper in this darkness feels unnecessary, as if the lack of sight is a constant reminder of how loud every sound actually is if you only listen.

"Please what?" he asks.

He wants me to beg. I pointlessly close my eyes, as if to hide from my own guilt. I don't feel guilt for my desperation, but I for my weakness, that I've come this far without telling him the single most important thing I came here to tell him. After all, what am I even doing if I don't think there's a future for us? *Using him.*

I shake my head as I wrestle with my own thoughts. No. I'm not just using him. I'm trying to explore the possibility that this could work, that maybe if he had more time with me he'd see I could be a woman he'd want to raise a family with. Or maybe I'm hoping when he learns I'm pregnant, he'll embrace the idea and want to raise the baby with me. He might even want more.

As much as I try, it all sounds thin, and my attempts to assuage my guilt are fruitless. Despite the almost mind-numbing *want* I feel to have him down to my core, I stand up awkwardly. I try to walk toward the wall where I hope I can find a light. I have to tell him or get away. I have to do something, but I can't just keep going like nothing is wrong.

"What are you doing?" he asks sharply.

"I need to go," I say.

Somehow he finds me immediately in the dark, gripping my arm tightly. "You're not going anywhere."

"Let me go," I say, tugging away.

I expect him to let me go free, but instead I feel the weight of his body push into me. We both fall backwards, and for a split second, I'm terrified of the impact I'll feel with the ground. Instead, we crash into the soft comforter of the large bed I was kneeling in front of when I came into the room. My legs are bent over the edge of the bed and Jayce's body is pressed to mine, keeping me in place. "I'm not going to let you go again, princess."

The safe words are on the tip of my tongue. Yellow. Red. One word and I'm almost certain he would let me go. Yet, I can't bring myself to say them. Instead, I just uselessly struggle against him, pushing at his strong body with no effect.

"You don't want me to let you go," he whispers into my ear, sucking my neck between his lips and running his tongue to my earlobe, where he bites hard enough to send a small tinge of pain through me. "I don't know why you think you need to run. I'll care later, but right now, all I know is there's only one way I'm not going to make you cum all over my cock--and that's if you say the safe word."

There it is. He couldn't make it any more clear, but I still can't bring myself to say the words. Deep down I know it's because he's right. I feel guilty. I feel wrong. But I want this too badly to summon that last bit of willpower to tell him to stop.

In my frustration--more with myself than him--I lash out, pushing and swatting at him. One of my wild movements in the dark catches his face. He pauses for a fraction of a second as if stunned that I'd be so bold. He grips my hips and heaves me farther onto the bed so my head lands on the pillows. I feel the bed sink as he climbs on after me with an almost frantic pace and flips me over so my stomach is pressed down into the comforter. With one rough motion, he yanks my legs open and lowers his body over me.

He thrusts his cock inside me without hesitation. I gasp, trying to reach back to press on his hips and slow him down, but he takes both my wrists in one hand and pins them down over my head and against the pillows, using his other hand to hold himself up as he starts working his cock into me with a pace that has my hands clenching around the pillows.

I'm powerless. Utterly out of control and completely at his mercy. I know I should feel something like fear or panic or maybe even anger, but I feel none of it. I'm overcome by a single, earth-shatteringly powerful emotion: *need*. It's as if every time I struggled in vein to resist a man and failed flashes before my eyes--all the times I was hurt and made to feel silly and stupid and ashamed. With Jayce, it's different. I struggled and fought, but with every movement of his body and thrust of his cock into me, pleasure floods my body, washing me over with what feels like pure, white ecstasy. He didn't wrestle control from me to hurt me like all the others before him. He took it from me to show me how wonderful I could feel if I let him own me.

Thrust by thrust, I feel the force bleed out of him until he's not fucking me like a disobedient submissive, but he's working himself into me with the passionate pace of a lover. His slides both hands up my wrists and threads his fingers through mine while his lips fall to my ear.

"I love you, Miley," he whispers. "Don't ever forget that."

My heart clenches, skin tingling all over even as my body jolts forward with each thrust of his hips. "I love you too," I say in a surprised voice. I'm surprised because I mean it. I didn't realize it until this precise moment, not completely. But now that the words have left my lips, I can feel how true they are. I love him. I love the way he came into my life and stood between me and all the things that would hurt me. I love how selflessly he protects me. I love the way I feel when he looks at me, when he touches me, and when he commands me to give myself to him.

I love being with him.

I open my eyes wide, and even though I can't see anything but the darkness, it feels like I'm seeing it all clearly for the first time. Maybe the first time ever.

The feelings mingle within me, swirling together with the pleasure, the sense of confinement, of surrender, and of being in his absolute control until it feels like it's building toward a crescendo that will leave me trembling and gasping for breath.

I squeeze his hands so hard I know it has to hurt, but he only holds on tighter, driving his length into me, rocking his hips until every last movement is pure euphoria.

I gasp out his name, not caring anymore if he'll punish me for calling him something other than Sir while he's taking me as my dom. I arch my ass up into him, begging for more of his cock even as my walls tighten around him. At the last second, he slides out of me and guides his cock up the crease of my ass until he tenses, releasing hot cum on my back.

I figured he put a condom on in the dark at some point, and the fact that he pulled out hits me like a brutal reminder of the space that still stands between us. I can love him all I want and he can be the most perfect man in the world for me, but there's nothing except a miracle that could bridge one of the most important gaps between us. I want kids. He doesn't.

I'm pregnant, and he has no idea.

I let my head sink into the comforter, fighting back tears of confusion and frustration. *Just tell him. Get it over with. Tell him the truth and stop being a coward.*

"Jayce..." I say.

He sighs, rolling over and laying beside me on the bed. "What is it, princess?" He punctuates his question with a tender kiss on my shoulder. The simple gesture holds so much love my heart practically bursts, even as it feels like it's about to break from telling him the truth.

"I'm pregnant," I say.

It feels like forever before he finally speaks. "You're sure?" he asks finally. There's no hint of emotion in his voice--only a calm, measured tone that betrays nothing.

"I'm pretty sure, yes," I say. "But even if I wasn't... I wanted to tell you since the party and I just didn't have the courage. I've always wanted kids."

He claps his hands twice, making me jump with surprise and then squint my eyes against the sudden flood of light.

"Wait a second," I say, shielding my eyes with my hand. "Your BDSM dark room had a freaking clap light?"

But I forget the ridiculousness of it in a moment when I see the look on his face. It's not what I expected. He's not angry, but he's not happy. There's an almost sad curl to his lips and angle of his eyebrows that takes me by surprise.

"Jayce?" I ask. "Can you please say something?"

"I'm sorry I did that to you," he says. "Fuck, I'm sorry."

I roll to my side so I can properly give him a full-dose of *what the hell did you just say?* The cum on my back gets on his comforter as I do, but that's the least of my worries right now. "You're *sorry*?" I ask.

He closes his eyes, breathing out a long, slow breath. He's wrestling with something internally, clearly searching for the right way to say what he's feeling.

"My mom died a few months after she had me. There was some complication with the pregnancy, so they had to perform a C-section. A few weeks later--I don't know exactly when because Leo only talked about it once, and even then he was sparse on details--some kind of infection set in from the surgery. She barely had enough to get by without our dad in the picture, so she didn't think she could afford to get treated for it I guess. But it cost her her life."

"I'm so sorry, Jayce," I say. My stomach twists as I start to piece together how that must have shaped him and changed his views on having children even before he tells me the rest. It starts to make sense, but only little by little, like pieces of a puzzle sliding together.

"I know it wasn't my choice. I know that," he says again more quietly, as if to himself. "But I've never been able to shake the sense of guilt, like it was my fault somehow. So any time I ever thought about what it'd be like to find the woman I love, I've always told myself I'd never get her pregnant. The risk is too great. It feels like such a selfish thing... wanting kids and forcing the woman I love to take that risk for me."

"Wait," I say, heart pounding. "So you *do* want kids?"

"God, yes," he says, lips flickering into a smile for an instant. "Yeah, I just always thought I'd end up adopting. Maybe. But yeah, as much as I know adoption is right and there are kids who need it, part of me still wanted this," he says, pressing a hand to my stomach so gently it makes my skin tingle. "I wanted to know the woman I'd spend the rest of my life with was carrying my child, that I'd marked her so permanently nothing on the Earth could ever fucking change it. She'd be mine, and so would her baby. But I could never make that decision knowingly. When I took you in the club that first night, I wasn't even thinking. I was so damn hungry to have you right then and there it was like my brain just shut off."

"I'm not going to get an abortion," I say firmly. He hasn't asked me, but it seems like he's dancing around the topic. On one hand, he says he wants this, but on the other he still seems to think the risk is too much. "I can't do that."

"I'd never ask you to," he says.

"Then why do you look so grim?" I ask, barely holding back tears. It feels like he's moments away from telling me he can't bear to be around it, or that this isn't a commitment he really wants.

He touches my cheek softly, staring into my eyes. "Sorry," he says. A grin splits his face. "I was just saying a silent prayer that it'd be a boy."

I put my hands to my face, smiling and laughing even though some confused part of me still feels like crying. "Seriously?" I ask, burying my face in his chest. "I thought you were going to break up with me and you were just trying to bargain with God for it to be a boy?"

"Break up with you?" he asks, kissing the top of my head. "So we *are* dating, then?"

I sigh, glaring up at him, but I can't even glare without smiling right now. The relief hasn't hit me completely, and I know it's going to come in waves. Even when I can tell the good news hasn't sunken in completely yet, I already feel so relieved and happy that I could jump up and down with excitement--if I wouldn't be mortified to do that while completely naked in front of Jayce, that is.

"We had better be," I say, biting my lip.

"As long as you promise Darla never comes on a date with us again," he says.

I laugh. "She wasn't that bad. Come on."

"It was like having the grim reaper along, or maybe just our own personal black rain cloud."

"You had better stop teasing her. I'll call her and tell her what you're saying. I swear I will."

"Not when I'm done with you. You'll be too exhausted to even dial her number."

I raise an eyebrow.

He rolls me over, pinning me down and planting his strong arms on either side of my head. "You thought you could just tell me you're pregnant and get away with getting fucked once? Princess," he says, voice growing slow and raspy. "I can cum inside that beautiful little pussy of yours again, and I'm not going to be satisfied until I do."

"I THINK THAT'S THE LAST BOX," I SAY TO DARLA, WHO IS SWEATING profusely--probably because she opted to wear a thick, black ankle-length dress and long sleeves when she knew she was coming to help me move.

"Remind me again why Mr. Perfect couldn't help with this? Or your stupid brother?"

I give her a wry smile. "Because it was only like four boxes and I didn't want to make Jayce miss work for that. And Kyle's upstate until the weekend visiting his new girlfriend's family."

She raises an eyebrow at me. "Jayce works?"

I sigh. "Yes, Darla. He... I don't know. He buys things, I guess. But he makes more money when he sells them later, or something like that."

She grins. "You don't even know what he does."

"He does *business*," I snap. She has a way of getting under my skin so quickly sometimes, but I'm always struggling not to smile even as I'm yelling back and forth with her. "He probably invests. You know, business kinda stuff."

"Right," she says dryly. "What you're saying is you've been too busy humping him like a rabbit to know what he does."

"I have not--" I start, except I guess for a guy I haven't known that long, we *have* had a lot of sex. But it's not like we don't talk, too. I already know him better than anyone I dated for months and months. I'm carrying his baby, too, if that counts for anything. "Just forget it. I don't need to know the details of his job. I know he's good to me and he takes care of me. That's enough."

Darla makes a gagging sound and rolls her eyes. "So is your friend, who took off work to come help you move four fucking boxes because you're Miss Pregnant Princess who can't lift a feather." She gives me the faintest hint of a smirk to take the bite out of her words before she walks the box out into the hallway.

I shake my head, smiling after her. It has been two weeks since I told Jayce I'm pregnant, and I think the freedom of having the truth out is finally starting to set in. He's already having me move in with him. We're together practically every single day, and instead of getting sick of him, it's like I keep getting more desperate to see him by the hour.

And right when I am starting to think things have taken a

turn for the better, I look up to the doorway and see Cade. His arms are crossed and his eyes are boring into me. He looks sober, too, which for some reason scares me more than if he were drunk.

"Going somewhere?" he asks.

My old instincts scream for me to cower, to back into a corner of the room and just let him do what he's going to do--whether it's hit me or yell at me or call me names. Then when it's all over, I can just try to bury it along with the rest of the bad memories. But for the first time in my life, something else stirs in me. I don't know where it comes from, but I feel a strong sense of *Hell no* that comes roaring up.

Hell no he's not going to abuse me again.

Hell no I'm not going to just let him get away with this.

Hell. No.

I discreetly pull my phone from my pocket, turning my back to him like I'm shooting off a text, but instead I dial 911. I put the phone on speaker in hopes that it'll pick up our voices, but mute the speaker on my end so Cade won't hear. "What do you want, Cade?" I ask, trying to sound bored.

"I want you. That's what I've always wanted," he says.

I act like I'm setting my phone down carelessly, but I make sure the receiver is aimed outward where it will have a better chance of picking up our voices. "I broke up with you," I say firmly. For once my voice doesn't shake. I don't feel like a cowering child beneath the huge shadow of my father. "It's over. It has *been* over, Cade. You need to leave."

He steps inside my apartment, eyes never leaving my face. "Leave? It sounds like I need to slap you around a little, maybe. You never were very good at listening until I fucked up that pretty face of yours with a bruise or two."

I take a step back from him, trying not to move too far from the phone as I struggle to think of a way to say my address without tipping him off that an emergency operator is listening in.

"That would be a bad idea, considering Jayce is just in the other room taking a nap."

I wait, hoping Cade will check the room and take the bait so I can quickly speak to the operator.

My stomach turns to ice when Cade pulls out a switchblade and clicks it open. "Good. Then I don't even have to wait to fuck him up, too. I'd tell you not to go anywhere, but I already know you're too fucking scared and weak to run away. Why don't you just wait here and cry while I go carve up your boyfriend?"

He stalks off toward the bedroom. I lean down and whisper my address into the phone as quickly as I can. "Please, I'm alone. Send help as soon as you can. I'm going to run outside but he'll come for me."

I grab my phone and head toward the door just as Cade swears and comes stomping back out after me. I'm already in the hallway and about to go down the stairs when he bursts out of the apartment and yells for me.

"Get the fuck back here, bitch!"

Not this time, asshole.

I tear down the stairs, nearly knocking Darla over as she is heading back up and mopping her brow with her sleeve. She raises her eyebrows. "Oh you can run like a lunatic but you can't carry a--"

She spots Cade coming for me, and I glance over my shoulder just in time to see her actually body check him to the side when he tries to push past her. She's probably a hundred pounds lighter than Cade, but he was moving fast enough that the shove makes him lose his balance and tumble down a few steps, dropping his knife before he gets his feet again.

"Help," I say quickly to a guy in his twenties who's coming in the main entrance of the apartment complex on his phone. He looks up and fails to take the situation in before I've already blown past him and Cade has shoved him to the side.

I swing the door open and run to the right, but instead of going anywhere, I tuck myself between the door and the building, holding onto the handle so the only way Cade will see me is if he turns around and presses his head to the wall once he's outside.

I hear his heavy footsteps come thumping out of the building and then falter a few steps after he has started in the direction he thinks I went. He's probably wondering how I could already be out of his view. The streets are always crowded though, and he must figure I'm hiding in the crowd, because I hear him push forward again.

As much as I want to stay hiding, I know the chances of anything happening to him are slim to none if he's not still after me when the police show up. It goes against every instinct I have, but I step out from behind the door and yell after him. "Hey, asshole!" I shout.

To my amusement, Cade turns around immediately, as if his identity as an asshole is so internalized that he reflexively answers to the name.

Some people in the crowd seem to notice, but no one actually does anything. Everyone is too busy trying to get to work or to class or wherever they're going, and now it probably looks like I'm the one who was antagonizing him.

I start running from him as fast as I can while having to shove through the packed street. I can't do it as fast as Cade though, who has the strength to physically shove everyone out of his way much more easily than me. A glance over my shoulder tells me he's almost caught up with me, but Darla is also rushing out of the apartment now, too, heading toward him.

Cade's hand grips my shoulder from behind and yanks me backwards.

"You should've stayed hidden, bitch."

"Hey," says a guy in an indignant voice, as if he's offended to hear Cade talk to me that way. But the guy doesn't even stop walking, like his angry glare and word were enough to assuage his guilt over doing nothing.

"The police are coming," I say to Cade as he drags me toward an alley between the apartment building and the highrise beside it. "They'll be here any second."

"Right," says Cade. "You never called the cops before. Why would you now?"

The sound of sirens makes him stop mid-step. He tilts his head, as if trying to make sure he's not hearing things.

"You're hearing what you think you are," I say triumphantly. "That's the sound of you being fucked."

"I'll just come back for you another time," says Cade, who shoves off me and starts trying to run.

Darla shows up behind him at just the right moment, pushing against his chest and trying to slow him down. "Not so fast," she grunts through gritted teeth as she tries to hold him from moving.

I run up behind him and pull on the back of his shirt.

He becomes more desperate, swinging at Darla and I in his haste to try to get away. People nearby finally start to notice something is wrong, and an athletic guy about Cade's height even steps in and pins Cade's arms to his side.

"The fuck you doing, man?" asks the guy.

Two officers come jogging toward us, which causes almost everyone on the street to stop now and watch the spectacle as red and blue lights wash over everything.

"You the one who called?" asks one of the officers, who glances toward my apartment building.

"Yes," I breathe.

The next few minutes play out like I'm watching from far away. I see them cuff Cade and the way he struggles and tries to headbutt the officers like some wild animal. I see them throw him in the back of their cruiser and drive off as an ambulance arrives for me. I try to tell them I'm fine, but the EMTs still insist on sitting me down and checking Darla and I over for injuries.

"Any pain here?" asks the woman examining me while I sit on the back of the ambulance.

"None," I say distantly.

Beside me, Darla is blushing furiously as a male EMT with dyed black hair, tattoos, and about fifty black wristbands is looking her over.

I can't stop thinking about how I actually did it. The old me would've become a victim to whatever Cade was planning. If I made it through, my brother or Jayce probably would've ended up taking their anger out on him in an attempt to protect me, but like always, the damage would've already been done. I would've had the same, lingering self-loathing that always comes after the abuse.

The oddest part is that even though Jayce wasn't here, I know he's the one who saved me. I'm the one who finally stood up for myself, but Jayce was the one who helped empower me. Strangely enough, it was surrendering to him that taught me how strong I really could be. I've been surrendering by instinct my whole life, and it was only when I learned to do it on purpose that I saw how to stand up.

JAYCE

All Miley's things are in my house now, and they barely take up a quarter of a room. I lean against the wall and look at the boxes and sparse bits of furniture that she has spent a lifetime accumulating. My little princess... I can't fucking wait to start spoiling you. She deserves so much more, and I'll make sure she has it.

She's in the kitchen now sipping on a hot chocolate. She tried to turn down the drink, but I thought she could use something comforting. Thinking of what she went through earlier today still makes me want to punch a hole through the wall. That, and I want to lock her up in my house where I can swallow her up in my arms, keeping her safe from all the shit out there. But then I guess I don't need to.

When she told me how she handled herself, I was so proud of her I could barely hold it in. I think back to the broken little bird I saw when she came to tell me about Cade that first night I met her. I knew she was strong and beautiful beneath the broken woman I saw, but I don't know if I ever even imagined she could pull off something so incredible. I wouldn't have blamed her if she spent her whole life carrying the scars of her past, but she's better than that. She overcame it all.

"Sorry," she says, sliding up beside me and threading her arm around mine to nuzzle against me. "I know it's a mess right now, but I'll get it all sorted out soon."

"No," I say. "You'll relax and enjoy yourself, because you don't need to be doing all that work." I put my hand on her still-flat stomach and grin. "We don't want to go shaking things up for our little boy and scaring him off."

She laughs. "You had better stop assuming it's a boy. I don't want you to find out it's a girl and be disappointed."

"I won't be. I'd love her just as much. Besides, it would mean we could keep trying for more."

She raises an eyebrow and turns to look at me sharply. "You'd be willing to have more? But I thought..."

"I know," I say. "What you did today though... You stopped letting your past control your present and I want to do the same. Besides, if I had known you were such a tough son of a bitch, I wouldn't have been worried about you making it through a pregnancy in good health."

She gives me a crooked smile. "What, so you thought I was a weak son of a bitch?"

I chuckle. "No. I thought you were delicate." I kiss her forehead. "You may be able to fight your own battles, but it doesn't mean you can't be pampered and spoiled from time to time--or all the time, if you let me."

She bites her lip and cuddles herself back into my arm. "I wouldn't complain about a little pampering."

"Good," I say abruptly. I lower my voice, which is a not-so-subtle way to remind her this request is coming from her dom. "Then go upstairs to the dark room. Get on your knees like before. You can leave your clothes on."

"Clothes on, sir?" she asks with a playful pout. "Are you sure?"

I grip her cheeks with one hand, letting the faintest shadow of my amusement show through. "You wouldn't question your dom, would you?"

"No, sir," she says.

"Then go."

She hurries upstairs, glancing back at me with an excited smile before she disappears up the stairs.

I had planned to wait a few more days, especially when I heard what happened today. But I can't wait any longer. When it comes to my princess, I have the patience of a child.

14

MILEY

I wait in total darkness on my hands and knees. The larger, circular room outside was so dark when I came in, I couldn't even see when I opened the door. So I did my best to crawl forward from memory, trying to get as close to the foot of the bed as I could. I'm wearing jeans today, which I hope won't be too hard for him to get off in the dark, but I'm sure he'll find a way. I have to admit I was hoping to see inside one of the other rooms next time he took me, but being taken in total darkness by him was such a thrill that I can hardly complain.

It's nearly five minutes before I hear the door open softly behind me.

"You may be wondering why we're using this room again before you've even seen the others," he says. "But it's because I have a surprise for you."

I raise my eyebrows, trying to imagine what kind of devious, kinky thing he could be hiding in the dark.

I almost scream when his hand gently comes down on my ass.

"Ah," he says. "There you are. Now I need you to obey me *exactly*. Do you understand?"

"Yes, sir," I say.

"Good. Crawl forward with one hand out-stretched until you feel the bed."

I do what he says a little awkwardly, almost losing my balance several times, but then I feel the comforter of the bed.

"Now," he says, "put your hand beneath the bed and feel around. *Carefully.*"

I do as he says, sliding my hand along the soft carpet until I feel something cold and metallic. I frown in the dark, running my fingers over it and picking it up. "A ring?" I ask, heart already pounding.

I clap my hands twice, jumping to my feet as I look at what's in my hands.

"Hey!" says Jayce. He's grinning wide and chuckling. "You're not supposed to clap on the lights yet."

"So punish me," I say through a broad smile. "Is this what I think it is?"

He comes closer, taking my wrists and kneeling. "Probably, unless you're thinking it's the prize out of a cereal box."

"That'd be some prize," I say, eyes already watering.

"Will you marry me?" he asks.

"Oh, let me think about that for a minute..." I say sarcastically. I lunge at him, wrapping my arms around him and crying into his neck. "Yes. This is crazy, but yes."

"Crazy would've been waiting another minute to ask you, princess. Now let me see how this looks on you," he says, gently pushing me back so he can slide the ring on my finger.

I sigh down at it in disbelief. It's obviously ridiculously expensive, but it's not so big that I look like a trophy wife or a gold-digger. It's exactly what I would've picked if price was no object. I just can't believe he already asked me. "What if you don't like the way I snore?" I ask. "Or how I can't seem to brush my teeth without getting water spots all over the mirror?"

He shrugs. "I'm a heavy sleeper, and I have a maid."

I give him a stern look. "A sexy maid?"

"Hmm," says Jayce, who makes a show of stroking his chin in thought. "I guess when he wears this one particular outfit, he does look pretty muscular."

"Oh my God," I say, slapping his arm. "You seriously have a male maid?"

"Yeah, his name is Jayce."

"Okay, now I *know* you're lying. There's no way you keep this whole place clean on your own."

"When I'm staying here, I do," he says. "Cleaning is my stress relief. I enjoy it."

"Wow," I say. "Are you sure someone didn't make you on an assembly line somewhere?"

"Hm," he says, reaching for the buttons of his shirt. "That's a good question. Why don't you give me a full body exam to look for a barcode."

15

EPILOGUE - JAYCE

Three years later

❧

The entire house smells like Thanksgiving. As a self-proclaimed disaster in the kitchen, I let Miley, Leo, and Lysa cook up the feast while I was left on baby wrangling duty. Leo's kids are content playing with the train set we have set up in the playroom, but Amelia is on some kind of mission where the only objective is to see how many ways she can *almost* off herself just before I save her. I lost count of how many times we narrowly avoided losing her today between the fact that she learned how to pull the child safety plugs out of the outlets and the unfortunate combination she has of loving heights and having no sense of balance.

"Daddy chase me!" she says happily as she weaves through the house and shows no signs of tiring despite what seems like the marathon of a chase she has led me on.

She has only really been talking for a few months now, but in the last few weeks it seems like she's learning a handful of new words a day and even stringing them together into sentences. I haven't gotten tired of hearing my little girl call me daddy yet. I think of how badly I thought I wanted her to be a boy and it seems unreal. I still want a boy, but I wouldn't trade Amelia for the world. She's my little girl, and if I had a boy like I thought I wanted first, we wouldn't have her.

I snatch her up and roll her into my arms, blowing raspberries on her belly until she giggles. "Hey," I say, kneeling down and setting her back on her feet. "Go tickle mommy's toes."

"Yeah," whispers Amelia, who waddles off toward the kitchen.

I only have to wait a few seconds before I hear Miley scream with laughter, followed shortly by Amelia's giggles.

It's only a half hour later when we've all sat down for dinner and have the kids at their own smaller table in the playroom so they can wander around and eat at their leisure--because when it comes to Amelia, there's no tying that little lady down in a high chair. She's a roaming eater and there's hell to pay if we try to take that freedom away from her.

Leo and Lysa sit across from Miley and I, while Lysa's mom, Rachel sits at the head of the table. Miley's brother Kyle and his girlfriend are on the other end of the table as well. As usual, Lysa's mom is glaring at Leo and I, but more of her glares go Leo's way. I've gotten to know her through the few times a year we all meet up for holidays now, and despite having some overwhelmingly off-putting qualities, like her tendency toward name calling, glaring, crude jokes, and aggressive finger poking, she's actually pretty nice to have around.

"We going to eat?" asks Rachel, "Or are we just going to eye-fuck the food all damn night?"

I cover my mouth, snorting out a laugh as Lysa gives her mom a look of disbelief. Leo doesn't even look phased, which is a testament to how used to her he has become. Miley gives me a subtle bulge of her eyes before she reaches to plate herself some food with a barely hidden grin.

Kyle nudges his girlfriend, who smirks up at him.

After dinner, we put on Aladdin for the kids, who surprise us by actually sitting down quietly to watch. Rachel literally fell asleep at the dinner table, where Lysa was nice enough to prop a pillow under her forehead while she sleeps off the bottle of wine she drank mostly by herself. I spend the entirety of the movie with Miley in my arms, running my fingers through her hair and across her back. I look between her and Amelia and think of how I never thought I'd deserve a life as good as this.

"I love you, princess," I whisper to her.

She looks up at me with those big, gorgeous eyes that only seem to get more beautiful every day. "I love you too. *Sir,*" she adds with a flirtatious wiggle of her eyebrows.

Fuck. I glance at the clock. Just a few minutes and we'll be kicking everyone out so we can get Amelia to bed. Just a few minutes before I can take her upstairs, but I don't think I can even wait that long...

16

EPILOGUE - MILEY

∽

Jayce announces to everyone that we'll be right back because we need to go clean up the kitchen before it starts to smell. It's an odd excuse, given that we already cleaned up most of the food, but everyone is too drowsy to seem to notice or care. If Darla had been able to come, I'm sure she would've had some sarcastic comment right about now, but she's still too obsessed with Matt, the dark haired EMT she met the night I got Cade arrested. She hasn't made much time to hang out with me since they got together, but I can't be too upset because she actually seems happy for once.

Jayce half-drags me through the kitchen, where he shakes a pot in the sink around for a few seconds and then takes me outside on the darkened patio by the pool.

"What are you doing?" I laugh.

"Shh," he says. We move outside and he doesn't waste any time pinning me to the wall of the house, just out of view from the windows. "What I'm doing," he whispers, "is fucking my dirty wife, who doesn't know better than to tempt me."

I close my eyes and lean my head back because I know how he loves to kiss my exposed neck. Just like I expect, the warmth of his mouth finds my neck and takes my breath away. "God," I gasp. "You always know exactly what I need."

"Quiet," he growls. "I don't want to have to fuck you in front of my brother, or yours."

I bite my lip to stay silent, but the idea that he needs to fuck me so badly even after he has had me so many times makes my heart flutter. "Then hurry up," I whisper in his ear teasingly.

He grunts, lifting me by my legs and pinning me harder to the wall. He pushes my dress up and pulls his pants down within seconds. In his hurry to have me, he just yanks my panties to the side and guides his cock in. I was worried I hadn't had enough time to get wet for him, but as usual, I'm already soaked after only a few words and a few moments of contact.

I squeeze my eyes shut, not even needing the extra layer of excitement BDSM brings, and apparently he doesn't either. Over the last couple years, I've found that sometimes we both seem to enjoy just normal, vanilla sex--though it always feels miles beyond *just sex* with Jayce. Whether he's binding me and punishing me or just holding me as he uses my body, there's a tender, possessive quality to his touch that only gets more addicting with time.

He treats me like his most prized possession, like the thing in the world he would do anything and everything to protect and keep. When I'm being held by him like this, even when he's driving his length into me again and again, drawing my orgasm closer with every thrust, my world feels right. I can feel his love for me in the way his fingers thread through my hair and he never seems to stop caressing and touching me, exploring my body like it's the first time he's ever felt me.

I'm his. He said it when we first met, and he has never stopped making me feel it. "Oh God," I whisper. "I'm going to cum."

"I fucking love you," he breathes into my ear. He tenses, filling me with his hot cum. My own climax comes as soon as I feel the kick of his cock inside me, making my walls tense and pulse, my whole body filling with a warm, fuzzy heat.

I slump back as he pulls himself out and slides back into his pants. All I have to do is shift my panties and shimmy my hips to fix my clothes. "There's something I want to tell you," I say, barely able to hold in my excitement. "I was going to try to wait until I was more sure, but I think I know. It feels the same as it did last time..."

Recognition sparks across his features. He frowns and smiles at the same time, lips parting into a confused smile.

"We're pregnant again. My period was due a few days ago and the tests are coming up positive already. I've already taken four."

Jayce picks me up like a sack of potatoes, throws me over his shoulder, and runs inside. I try to tell him to stop being a maniac and put me down, but he doesn't hear me because he's already shouting the news to everyone. "We're pregnant!" he yells as we come around the corner into the living room.

Everyone looks up at us, but Rachel is the first to speak. "I think you've got to give it more time than a few seconds to happen, hotshot." She winks knowingly.

My cheeks flush red to think that Rachel knew what we were out there doing.

"No," says Jayce, who's clearly too excited to get her joke. "She already took four tests. All positive!"

"I guess we're telling everyone," I say a little sarcastically. I'm not irritated though. I've never been much for keeping secrets like this--except when I thought Jayce was going to hate me for being pregnant, at least. I definitely didn't keep it a secret when I got word that Cade was going to be behind bars for at least fifteen years because two other women came forward about the way he abused them. "Could you put me down now?" I ask.

Jayce seems to realize he's still hoisting me on his shoulder and eases me to the ground.

"Baby?" asks Amelia.

"Yes, sweetie!" I say scooping her up and hugging her tightly. "You're going to have a little sister or brother."

"Brother," says Jayce. "Definitely a brother. Or mommy's not done getting pregnant."

ALSO BY PENELOPE BLOOM

Thanks for reading Knocked Up and Punished! Don't forget to join my mailing list if you haven't already! You an sign up through my Facebook Page online!

xoxo,

Penelope

More by Penelope Bloom

Knocked Up by the Master (#12 ranked Amazon Bestselling novel for October)

Knocked Up by the Dom (USA Today Bestselling Novel and #8 ranked Bestselling Amazon novel for September)

(The Citrione Crime Family)

His (Book 1)

Mine (Book 2)

Dark (Book 3)

Punished (*Amazon top 40 Best Selling Novel for February* Standalone BDSM Romance)

Single Dad Next Door (*Amazon top 12 Best Selling Novel for February*)

The Dom's Virgin (*Amazon top 22 Best Selling Novel for March)

Punished by the Prince (*Amazon top 28 Best Selling Novel for June)

Single Dad's Virgin (*Amazon top 10 Best Selling Novel for April)

Single Dad's Hostage (*Amazon top 40 Best Selling Novel for May)

The Bodyguard

Miss Matchmaker

Made in the USA
San Bernardino, CA
18 November 2017